Five Guns South

They had robbed and pillaged their way through a whole territory by the time they hit the mountains. But the five raiders, led by Luke Quantril, were saving their cruellest heist for the quiet town of Bandyrock as they plotted their escape south.

Here, they would hold the town brutally to ransom until they had drained it of every last dollar before heading for the border with trailed hostages at their mercy. Then it would be left to Sheriff Connell and a greenhorn posse to pursue the raiders across the searing desert in a bid to seek raw retribution in the name of justice.

Much blood would be spilt before peace finally came to a troubled land.

By the same author

Rain Guns
Hennigan's Reach
Hennigan's Law
Shadow Hand
Bloodline
The Oldster
Border Kill
Bitter Sands
Go Hang the Man
Gun Loose
Drift Raiders
Trail Breaker
Shoot to Live
Plains' Wolf
Small-Town Gun
McKenna's Mountain

Five Guns South

DAN CLAYMAKER

A Black Horse Western

ROBERT HALE · LONDON

© Dan Claymaker 2004
First published in Great Britain 2004

ISBN 0 7090 7549 9

Robert Hale Limited
Clerkenwell House
Clerkenwell Green
London EC1R 0HT

This one for K and P
who knew the value of the journey

Typeset by
Derek Doyle & Associates, Liverpool.
Printed and bound in Great Britain by
Antony Rowe Limited, Wiltshire

ONE

It was first light through a cloud-cover clearing on a brisk wind when the five riders, their long coats billowing behind them like wings, broke from the dirt drift and reached an outcrop of pine at the foot of the hills.

They reined their snorting, lathered mounts to a halt and sat for a while in silence, watchful of the trail they had just left, uncertain of the lands still to come. It was the heaviest, deepest-weathered of the five who finally spoke.

'We're clear. There ain't nobody followin'.' Luke Quantril spat out the words as if cleansing his mouth of troublesome grit, relaxed his shoulders and wiped the dirt from his face. 'So where in hell are we?' he growled, his gaze shifting to the oldest of the group, a ruddy-faced, wet-eyed man sporting a battered derby on his head and a spotted bandanna at his neck. 'What you reckon, Prof?'

Ezra Markham, known to the others as Professor, grumbled at the back of his throat as he fumbled in the depths of his coat pocket.

'South,' he announced, unfolding a sheet of parchment across his mount's neck. He studied the sheet for a moment, a grubby finger tracing the line of a trail. 'Bluespeck Hills comin' up,' he continued, lifting his gaze to the range ahead. 'Clear them and it's a mite short of a hundred miles to the border.'

Jason Stock, a lean, younger man with dark narrowed eyes and a fringe of matted hair below the brim of his hat, whistled through his teeth.

'A hundred miles,' he echoed ahead of an aimed fount of spittle. 'That is some distance.'

'Too far for you, boy?' tittered Rimms McCane, easing to the shift of his snorting mount. 'T'ain't goin' to look good for you if you don't make it.'

'Who said anythin' about not makin' it?' snapped Stock, his lips tightening, eyes darkening. 'You sayin' as how—'

'Cut it,' clipped Charlie Loome, running a soothing hand across his gut to raise a rumbling belch. 'This ain't the time or the place for pride-pickin'. We got decisions to make.'

'Too right we have,' said Quantril, wiping his face again. 'Spell it out, Prof. Let's be hearin' the reckonin'.'

'Choices are in short supply,' began the old man, folding the parchment carefully. 'Fact is, we've got only one: we stay headin' south. We need the border, sooner the better.'

'I'll go along with that,' said McCane, scanning the grey bulk of the hill range. 'We goin' over them?' he asked. 'T'ain't goin' to be easy.'

Prof cleared his throat. 'Over 'em, through 'em, don't matter none. We clear the Bluespecks then head for Bandyrock.'

'Bandyrock?' Loome winced on another belch. 'If that's what I think it is – some mangy dirt town back of nowhere – then I ain't for it. We stay out of towns. Give 'em a wide berth, leastways for the time bein'.'

'He's got a point there, Prof,' said Quantril.

'I'll say he's got a point,' gestured Stock, snapping the reins to his mount through his twitchy fingers. 'One helluva point. We so much as set a foot in a town, we're askin' for trouble, lookin' down the barrel of it. You bet. News travels fast, and news of what we've left behind is goin' to set us up for the first noose goin'. You bet to that too. No, I ain't for no towns.'

'No choice,' grunted Prof, patting the parchment back to his pocket. 'No choice because we're broke. Clean out of money. Not a dollar worth speakin' to. And we need money, real money, if we're goin' to make reachin' the border worth the ride.'

'That's fool talk—' began McCane.

Quantril growled for silence. 'Hold on. Let's hear what Prof's figurin'.'

Prof adjusted his battered derby and tweaked the folds of the spotted bandanna.

'Yeah, well you'd best listen, and listen good, 'cus we're talkin' survival here, and it ain't for bein' taken lightly.' He grumbled at the back of his throat, shrugged his shoulders and watched the others through his wet, red-rimmed eyes. 'T'ain't of no use crossin' the border, if we're crossin' it broke. That's fryin' pan to fire. No prospect. Only way the likes of us are goin' to make anythin' worthwhile of that Southern livin' is with money.'

'Damnit, we had money,' spat McCane. 'A whole

bankload of the stuff.'

'You bet we did,' continued Prof with another tweak of the bandanna. 'Most of what the First National's vaults at Morristown were holdin'.' He paused a moment. 'Had it, then blew it on that drinkin', gamblin', womanizin' shenanigans at Gentry.'

'You did your share, old man!' quipped Loome.

'Ain't sayin' I didn't,' said Prof, 'and mebbe it wouldn't have mattered a jot if we hadn't got to shootin' up the sheriff before we left.'

'That was a mistake,' mused McCane.

'All-time mistake,' added Stock.

Prof grunted. 'And we all had a finger on the trigger, remember that.'

There was a moment of silence as the riders reflected on a town, the faces in it, a time past.

'We should've kept ridin' after that,' murmured Stock. 'Just kept ridin'. . . .'

'But we didn't, did we?' added Prof. 'And that was another big mistake.'

Loome ran a hand over his stubble.

'That woman was askin' for it,' he croaked.

'Didn't have to kill her, did you?' growled Prof. 'Didn't have to gun her old man. We didn't have to torch the homestead, did we? In hell's name, we only stopped to water the horses, beg ourselves a plate of beans. 'Stead of that—'

'That's enough,' snapped Quantril, cracking reins between his fingers. 'We all know what happened. Don't need no remindin', and you've made your point, Prof. If I'm readin' you right, you're sayin' we need to give this Bandyrock place a look over with a view to it bank-rollin' us on to the border before whoever might be hard on our heels gets any closer. That about the way of it?'

'That's exactly the way of it,' said Prof. 'There's almost certain to be somebody trailin' us. So far we've stayed ahead, but we can double our edge if we cross the Bluespecks at a pace and avail ourselves of whatever hospitality Bandyrock's got to offer. It's the nearest town, and mebbe the last chance we'll get in that push for the border.' He patted the battered derby. 'Like I say, no choice.'

'Well,' asked Quantril, 'we all agreed – we head for Bandyrock?'

Charlie Loome spat. 'Bandyrock it is,' he muttered reluctantly.

Rimms McCane scanned the grey cloud-smothered hill range.

'That's goin' to be one helluva ride. One helluva ride.'

Jason Stock reined his mount to the trail.

'Let's hit it,' he mumbled.

Minutes later the long coats were billowing again as the five riders headed due south.

TWO

Sheriff Frank Connell relaxed in the chair on the veranda fronting his office, tipped his hat against the glare of the mid-morning sun and stretched his long, lean legs to their full length. Quiet – beautifully, peacefully quiet, just the way he liked it on a hot summer's day. Nobody of note about, no good reason to be about at this stifling hour; nobody expected, nobody wanted come to that, and the promise of a gentle afternoon to the cooler shade of an equally peaceful evening. Perfect.

Could he ask for more? No, he could not, nor would he. Bandyrock was precisely his measure, tailor-made to both his immediate needs and his longer term aspirations. He could live with this town, in this state at this pace, for as long as its good folk deemed him worthy.

He smiled softly to himself beneath the broad brim of the tilted hat. Not that he had always had it so easy. Nothing like, now he came to recall. Kimberly had been no place for the squeamish, not even all those years back when the territory was opening up and the genuine settlers thin on the ground. Just about every scumbag, loose drifter, opportunist gunslinger and plain no-good sonofabitch had found his way through its streets – and invariably into the jail back of Sheriff Skinner's office where Connell had stood as a deputy.

Tough years, gritty years, a no holds barred, no quarter given or expected passage of time which, when he came to reflect on it, he would not have missed for a saddlebag of gold. He had eventually left to cross the Bluespeck Hills for his new post as sheriff of Bandyrock a tougher, wiser man with a sharp eye and a fast gun – the latter, he smiled again, being just about the least of his priorities in this town where he had not had cause to draw a gun, let alone fire it, in close on two years.

Like he always said, a quiet town, a nobody, nowhere place where a man might look to his gentle years with an easy mind.

He shifted and adjusted his hat at the creak and grind of an approaching wagon.

'Good day to you, Sheriff,' called Jake Wardman, reining his outfit to a halt facing Connell. 'And a warm one too,' grinned the man, mopping his brow with a bandanna.

'Say that again,' said the sheriff. His gaze narrowed against the glare. 'How's things back at your spread? Still raisin' them hogs? See you've been stockin' up.'

'Three months' supplies here, Mr Connell. Shan't be seein' town again 'til the first rains. It's back to the Bluespecks and the hogs. Don't reckon they'll ever make me a fortune, but they're a livin'.'

'How's the family?'

Jake pushed his hat to the back of his head.

'Well, now, Mr Connell, would it surprise you to know that darn near a half of what I'm cartin' here is women's doin'?'

11

'How come?' frowned Connell.

'Martha's gotten it into her head that it's time she had some new fancy-frilled dresses. Can't fathom on why. Looks as good to me as the day I wed her. And you know what, darn me if that flighty daughter of mine, young Jessie, ain't bitten by the same bug! Would you be believin' it? Just about cleared old Wheeler's store of cloth and cottons, needles and buttons and bows. . . .' Jake settled his hat again with a flourish. 'What would you make of that, Mr Connell? Them women of mine reckon for me bein' made of money or somethin'?'

'And worth every cent, I'll wager,' grinned the sheriff. 'They're hard workin' gals. 'T'ain't easy makin' a livin' out of hog-farmin'. Give 'em a treat. They deserve it!'

'I ain't sure whose side you're on here,' groaned Jake.

'I ain't takin' sides,' gestured Connell. 'You just make sure you bring Martha and young Jessie to town on your next visit – and both in their new dresses.'

'I'll do that, Mr Connell,' smiled Jake. 'You bet I will. Show 'em off, eh? Well, that's a promise. Three months from today.' He flicked the reins and called to the team to move on. 'See you around, Sheriff.'

Connell raised a hand in farewell, slumped back in the chair, stretched his legs and tipped his hat against the still-dazzling glare. The sounds of Jake Wardman's wagon making its slow way back to the spread in the folds of the Bluespeck Hills gave way to the lazy buzz of a sleepy fly.

A quiet town with quiet folk leading quiet lives, he mused again, where the event of the year would undoubtedly be the sight of Martha Wardman and her daughter in their new dresses.

*

12

The riders led by Luke Quantril were two days into the Bluespeck Hills when Charlie Loome's guts finally erupted in a bout of violent sickness and they were forced to let him rest at the side of a creek stream.

'Never could hold his liquor,' quipped Jason Stock cynically as he flicked a pebble to the trickling flow and gave the sleeping body of Loome no more than a cursory glance.

'That ain't liquor gripe,' said McCane. 'Mebbe he's gotten a fever. Mebbe it's got somethin' to do with these godforsaken hills.' He gazed miserably over the sprawl of the peaks, the reaches of rock and skeletal scrub, the meandering emptiness of the track they had been following. 'We any closer to seein' the back of this hell-hole?' he asked, the gaze shifting to Prof. 'What's that map of yours tell you?'

'Not a deal,' said the old man without bothering to take the document from his pocket. 'We just keep movin' south, same track, same pace, 'til I say other. There ain't no shortcuts to crossin' the Bluespecks. We'll be out of 'em when we're out of 'em. Can't say fairer.'

'Some prospect,' groaned Stock, flicking another pebble.

'Patience, fellas, patience,' shrugged Quantril. 'Somethin' we've been in short supply of lately. We've gotta learn to take things as they come. That way we don't go makin' mistakes. So it's easy go, nice and gentle. We'll clear these hills soon enough.'

'And then we've got Bandyrock,' murmured McCane, relaxing on one elbow. 'What we goin' to do

13

when we ride in there? Rattle a beggin' bowl? Rob a bank – assuming, o'course, they got a bank? Or mebbe we should go help ourselves. Hell, I'm sure the folk of Bandyrock are goin' to see the five of us a worthy cause!' He scraped a boot heel through the rock shale.

'Ain't no need for grousin' talk like that,' snapped Quantril. 'You had your share of the heist at Morristown. You had your fun at Gentry. You ain't got no cause to complain.'

'I ain't complainin',' said McCane, wide-eyed. 'I'm just askin' in the interests of my future.'

Stock tittered to himself behind a raised hand.

'Who says you've got a future, Rimms?' he grinned. 'I ain't seein' it from where I'm sittin'.'

Charlie Loome squirmed and moaned, his clasped hands cradling the rolls of his stomach.

'And what we goin' to do about him, f'cris'sake?' griped McCane with a nod of his head. 'Ain't he holdin' us up some? Ain't we wasted enough time here? Hell, who's to say there ain't somebody ridin' within a spit of our butts right now? Could be watchin' from any one of them peaks up there.'

'There ain't nobody sittin' on our butts or watchin' from any peak,' said Prof flatly. 'I know. I been listenin' *and* I've been keepin' my eyes open.' He patted the creases of the battered derby. 'We're alone – for now. But I ain't takin' it as a permanent state. There'll be somebody back there, just as there's always somebody up front. So we shift. Now. Trouble with Charlie here, he's hungry. He needs to eat. We all do. So let's find some place we can do just that.'

But it was to be another full day before the five

14

riders came within sight of the slow curl of smoke reaching from a homestead stack in a valley still some miles ahead.

THREE

'It was talk, only talk, but there ain't no smoke without fire is what I always hold to.' Doc Merry tapped the bowl of his pipe in the palm of his hand and blew the loose ash to the street. 'I ain't sayin' as how the fella had all the facts, but he sure as hell weren't spinnin' no yarn.'

Bernard Wheeler, storekeeper and unofficial town mayor, nodded thoughtfully, examined a button on his tailored frock-coat and cleared his throat.

'Wouldn't like to say one way or the other. Couldn't anyhow. But Doc's word is good enough for me. If the tale them travellin' folk told him out there on the Wittock Trail is only half of what really happened – and embellished some at that – then there's been one helluva time out Morristown way.'

The gathering of men taking in the cooler night air on the boardwalk at the Split Spurs saloon a week later murmured their agreement. A cloud of cigar, cheroot and pipe smoke drifted through the lantern glow like a clambering of moths. Somewhere in the bar behind them a man tinkled lazily on a worn piano. A girl giggled. Glasses clinked. The batwings creaked open.

'Ah, Sheriff Connell,' Wheeler smiled. 'You heard

16

this tale Doc's been tellin' us? Concerns some robbery at Morristown. That should interest you.'

'I've heard and I'm interested,' said Connell, joining the group of men 'Don't ever pass up a chance of hearin' what's been goin' on, but a bank robbery at Morristown is way off the trail to Bandyrock. I'd reckon for the robbers bein' well clear by now if that's what's troublin' you.'

'That's mebbe so, Sheriff,' said Adam Levens, pulling the folds of his blacksmith's apron into place, 'but accordin' to what them travellers told Doc, the scumbags – five of 'em – headed on to Gentry. That's where they killed the sheriff. Shot him in a drunken brawl or somethin'.' Levens folded his arms across his barrel chest. 'Gentry's a whole sight closer than Morristown.'

'Sure it is,' piped a man in the shadows, 'but that ain't to say as how we should worry. Types like them sonsofbitches ride fast and hard from law trouble. So where'd you figure for them headin', Mr Connell?'

'Well, now,' said the sheriff, taking his time to light a cheroot, 'in my experience I'd be reckonin' on the robbers headin' west. Plenty of solid mountain cover out that way. They'd be lookin' to go deep, hole up tight 'til the chase cools some. Give it a few weeks, mebbe a couple of months, and they could be out as far as Oregon, lost from sight in any one of a dozen settlers' townships come winter.' He blew a thin shaft of smoke. 'Yep, that's where the rats will be – somewhere out West.'

'That's a reassurin' thought, Sheriff.' Wheeler grinned. 'Guess we can all sleep easy in our beds, eh?'

The batwings to the bar swung open as proprietor Jay Matlan beamed his way to the boardwalk behind a

17

swirling cloud of cigar smoke.

'And amen to that! You bet! But no takin' yourselves off this early, fellas. There's a round of drinks
standin' on the bar. Follow me!'

Doc waited for the boardwalk to clear before
moving quietly to Sheriff Connell's side.

'You weren't serious with all that talk of Oregon, were
you?' he murmured, his gaze narrowed on Connell's
face. 'Them travellin' folk I encountered out there were
pretty certain: nobody knows for sure where the five
scum headed out of Gentry. And with the killin' of a
lawman on their backs, they weren't goin' to announce
it, were they? They could've headed anywhere. But
you're thinking what I'm thinkin', aren't you?'

Connell waited for another shaft of smoke to disappear on the night.

'That bein'?' he asked, without looking at Doc.

'If I were on the run out of Gentry and lookin' to melt
clean out of sight for a while, I wouldn't head west.' Doc
eased a half step closer to the sheriff. 'I'd head south. I'd
be lookin' to bury myself somewhere in the Bluespecks
'til I judged it safe enough to make for the border.' He
paused a moment. 'How would you rate my chances?'

'Better than most,' said Connell, his gaze still fixed on
the night. 'In fact, you'd stand a good chance of makin' it.'

Doc grunted his satisfaction. 'That why you're fillin'
them fellas back there with that talk of Oregon? You
figure it a fifty-fifty chance them scumbags might have
done just as I've said and headed for the Bluespecks?
And if they have, if they have ... Bandyrock could
easily be the next place to hole up. Right?'

Connell finished the cheroot and ground the butt

18

under his heel.

'Anythin's possible, Doc, you know that better than most. But I ain't for havin' this town gettin' jumpy for no good reason. There ain't a grain of evidence to show as how the Morristown robbers are headed this way, or within fifty miles of Bandyrock.'

'But you can't be saddle-tight sure, can you?' persisted Doc.

'No, I can't,' murmured Connell. 'Not for sure I can't.' He stared into the darkness for a moment. 'Them travellin' folk you encountered mention any names?'

Doc scratched his chin. 'We talked for close on an hour. I'd been out to the Beattie home takin' a look at Mrs Beattie who's expectin' her fifth when these folk – two wagons and teams – reached the Wittock Trail headin' due north, plannin' on makin' it to Red Rocks in three days. They'd heard of what had happened at Morristown and Gentry from a bunch of high plains drifters, so I guess I was gettin' the news third or even fourth hand. Names weren't mentioned, save one. His name came up two or three times. Quantril. Just that . . . Quantril. It ring any bells?'

The sheriff was a long ten seconds before he answered.

'You do me a favour, Doc?'

'Sure, if I can.'

'Keep an eye on the town tomorrow. I reckon I might just ride out and take a look around.'

'Any particular place?'

Connell half-turned to stare into the dark emptiness beyond the soft glow of lanterns.

'The Bluespecks,' he murmured.

FOUR

The early morning air was thinner and cooler as Sheriff Frank Connell reined to a softer, gentler pace through the thickest of the pines. He had saddled up the black mare and left town at the first hint of light, anxious to be clear of the main trail and into the shadowy cover of the foothills before full dawn. Now, easing back in the saddle and giving the mare a looser rein, he was able to begin watching, listening, taking in the very different and private world of the Bluespecks.

A man could ride into these hills and be as good as off the face of the earth in no time, he reflected. A man on the run could be buried in minutes and able to survive with ease. He could live out a dozen years among the crags and crevices, hidden valleys, secret creeks and darkened gulches, without fear of being disturbed let alone discovered. There was food to be hunted, water in the creek streams, shelter among the rocks. Here, in the Bluespecks, a man could disappear if he had reason enough to want to.

But could five men?

He murmured softly to his thoughts and trickled the reins through his fingers. Doc Merry's mention of the name Quantril had been the last thing he had wanted to hear in connection with the robbery at Morristown and the shooting at Gentry.

Luke Quantril was bad news at any time in any circumstances, but Quantril on the run, with almost certainly the infamous Prof Markham at his side, was a loose-reined disaster that could erupt anywhere, and would. Connell knew, he had seen it before, long years back when Quantril and Prof had first teamed up out St Louis way. It had been an evil match from the outset: robbery, pillage, looting and torching wherever they happened to fetch up and could raise the hungry guns to join them. There had been no shortage of recruits.

But who had Quantril and Prof been riding with through Morristown and Gentry? Was it possible that Quantril had opted to head south, probably on the advice of Prof who was always rattler-sharp when it came to doing the unexpected? Were they here now, somewhere deep in the sprawling silence and safety of the Bluespecks, and if they were, who in tarnation would know?

There was one man who might, thought Connell, reining the mare to the narrow track to the right.

Jake Wardman had spent the better part of his working life up here in the Bluespecks, had wed and raised his daughter in the valley homestead, and had once been described by Doc Merry as being the only man he knew who could talk to the hills and hear them answer.

Connell just hoped Jake had been listening real close of late.

The morning light an hour later was clear and bright, the sun high in the blue washed sky, the flies buzzing and dancing and a lone hawk circling hungrily, when Sheriff Connell at last urged the black mare the few yards to the ridge overlooking the valley.

Aware that the Wardmans would not be expecting visitors at this hour, if at all in such a remote spot, Connell already had an arm half raised to signal his approach as he topped the ridge.

He lowered it again as if it were no longer a part of him. A sickening chill gripped in his stomach. His blood ran as suddenly icy as a mountain stream. His stare became fixed and unblinking, and the stench of burning death and devastation irritated at his nostrils like blown dust.

He groaned at the sight of the torched and blackened homestead, the charred timbers, scattered furniture, pots, pans, bedding, stores, tools, a roll of the new dress fabric Jake had bought in town; swallowed on a parched, tensed throat at the sight of the smashed hog-pens, the broken bales, upturned feed troughs, tossed aside crates and timbers.

He reined the wide-eyed mare forward on a slow, measured pace, easing down the dry scrub slopes to the valley floor as if in a drifting veil of the shimmering heat. His gaze began to scan swiftly, left to right, taking in the scene in a jumble of images, the silence of the place seeming to shout in his ears.

It was the echoing call of the lone hawk that

brought him to a halt. He slackened the reins, patted the mare's neck, then slid slowly, smoothly from the saddle, almost in dread of putting a foot to the ash-grey ground. He moved forward carefully, swallowing, beginning to sweat yet still conscious of the chill at his spine, the cold, hollow prospect of what he knew he was about to find.

He groaned again, this time with a retching surge of breath as he came to the half-naked body of Martha Wardman. The Lord alone knew how long she had suffered before her attackers had finally knifed her and left her to rot like so much trash.

He stepped back, a sudden sickness welling in him, then an anger that made him kick viciously at a charred splinter of timber. *Hell!* he mouthed – and again, a dozen times until his mouth seemed filled with the curses.

He spun round, his eyes wild and anxious. Where was Jake? Where was Jessie?

He stumbled away through the debris, scrambling blindly now for anything that might give a hint of the fate of the girl and her father, the chilling realization beginning to dawn that the devastation and cold-blooded abuse and murder of Martha Wardman had been the doing of Luke Quantril and those riding with him.

But an hour's frantic search revealed nothing of the bodies and nothing save the scuffed hoof-prints of the attackers' mounts, to indicate where Jake and Jessie, dead or alive, might have been taken.

Kidnapped, he pondered, staring into nowhere? Why, to what end? The attack might bear all the brutal marks of Quantril's doing, but kidnapping was not his style. He kept life simple – take what you needed where you found it at whatever the cost. He did not clutter his thinking with hog farmers and their adolescent daughters, no matter how good-looking the daughter might be.

But what of those riding with him?

Connell had taken close on another hour to dig a decent grave for Martha and say a few words over her. It was as Jake would want, he figured. The spread had been her life and whatever the gruesome circumstances of her death, she would have wanted to be put to her rest on the land.

The sun was still high and fierce, the sky its cloudless blue when Connell took his last look round the devastation before reining the black mare back to the slope. He was leaving the valley with the chill still in his bones, the cold sweat beading on his brow and his thoughts already churning through the fate of Jake and Jessie and the nightmare reality of Quantril and his men being this close to Bandyrock.

He would raise a posse once back in town to go in search of Jake, get the townsfolk organized and aware of what might be heading their way, then send word through somehow to Morristown or Gentry for help. Do something, anything.

'Hell!' he cursed again as the lone hawk finally swooped to the lifeless valley.

FIVE

'I say we kill him. Right now. Here. Hang him. He ain't no use to us. Who's goin' to give a bent dollar if he lives or dies? So I say kill him.' Rimms McCane spat into the scrub, leaned back on one elbow and eyed the others with a half-grin creasing his sweat-streaked face. 'Don't tell me you ain't got the stomach for it, not after what we did back there.'

Jason Stock tittered, wiped the back of his hand across his mouth and continued to pick at his teeth.

Charlie Loome grunted, belched and closed his eyes. 'Might be as well to put the fella out of his misery seein' as how he's lost most of all he had.' His eyes opened slowly. 'Mebbe we should've finished him back there with his missus.' He belched again and groaned. 'I say we just get to leavin' these goddamn hills behind us soon as we can – with or without the old man. It don't fuss me none.'

Luke Quantril turned his weary gaze on Jake Wardman roped to a nearby tree in the shaded clearing where the riders had halted. He held it for a moment, then stared at Jessie, tied hand and foot at

25

her father's side, her eyes wide with fear, her long yellow hair matted across her shoulders, her working smock torn and smeared. She shivered and shuddered in spasms that racked her whole body.

'The old man lives,' pronounced Prof without lifting his eyes from the parchment map spread across his knees.

'How'd you reckon that so fast?' quipped Loome.

'He's of value breathin'; he ain't worth nothin' dead. Simple enough. We keep all our assets 'til we've got what we need out of Bandyrock. Then you can hang him, the girl along of him if you've a fancy for it.'

McCane spat into the dirt again.

'You've been busy there figurin' this through, so what's the deal?' he drawled, doing nothing to hide the resentment in his tone. 'We've got the old man, we've got his daughter. Hostages – right? Right, so we trade 'em in Bandyrock. But for what? How? When? I don't see—'

'Sometimes a helluva lot you don't see or figure, Rimms,' cracked Quantril, his gaze suddenly alight and fixed. 'Best listen up, eh? That way you'll mebbe get to learnin' some.'

McCane relaxed on his elbow, a scowl darkening his face.

'Nothin' complicated,' said Prof, setting aside the parchment. 'I ain't for taxin' your brains.'

'Well, thank the Lord for that!' smirked Stock.

Prof fiddled for a moment with the spotted bandanna. 'Puttin' it in a tin mug in one, we've got five pockets to fill with all the cash we can raise between here and the border. Once into Mexico and

26

we're ridin' dirt country for a helluva long way. Only fella with any standin' in them circumstances is the one with money. Very well . . .' He paused to tap his derby. 'Thinkin' it through, and reckonin' to my judgement of towns the likes of Bandyrock, there'll be enough money there to meet our immediate needs in full.'

'We sell the old man and the gal back to the town?' said Loome, stifling a hissing belch.

'Trade them, my friend,' grinned Prof. 'We take all they've got, all we need, in return for their lives. And they'll pay, make no mistake about that, particularly for the girl, who we don't finally release, of course, until we're well clear of the town and safe.'

'Damnit, why not ride in and take what we want?' grunted McCane, flicking pebbles to the scrub. 'We've done it often enough before. What about back there at the hog spread?'

'Because that way we'd only get what we see: the pickin's,' said Prof. 'We need more than crumbs. We need the whole darned meal, everythin' the town's got, down to its last dollar. And we need to take it without any lootin', torchin', pillagin' or murderin' – 'ceptin', of course, where necessary. You've had your fill of them for now. This we do quietly, efficiently, if you know what that means.' He began to fold the parchment map. 'I want to drain Bandyrock dry of all its money. We ride out for the border leavin' it empty.'

Quantril came to his feet, stretched and hitched his pants.

'That clear enough for you?' he growled, looking round the faces. 'You understand? Good. So now we

27

get busy. We head direct for Bandyrock, no more than a day's ride away. That so, Prof?'

'Correct. And the sooner we're movin' the better.'

'You ain't goin' to get away with this,' shouted Jake, straining against the ropes binding him. 'Not no how you ain't. I'll make sure of that! See you in hell first!'

'Somebody go shut that old gopher up, will yuh?' groaned Loome.

'My pleasure.' Stock beamed, springing upright. 'And while I'm at it, I'll just check on that pretty little mare there. Yeah, I'll do that.'

'You go easy,' ordered Quantril sharply. 'She's valuable.'

'You bet she is.' Stock smiled and sauntered towards the shivering girl.

'That fella worries me,' murmured Loome. 'He really does worry me.'

Bernard Wheeler walked the length of the boardwalk fronting his store and glared into the shimmering sunlight. He gripped the lapels of his coat, shook his head slowly and turned to cast his long shadow back towards the men watching him.

'Only one thing we can do,' he croaked hoarsely. 'There ain't no choice. We owe it to Jake and his missus.'

'I wouldn't expect you to think other, Bernard,' said Doc Merry, 'but I ain't sure as how you're right.'

The town men gathered behind him murmured their understanding.

'Gettin' lead-happy against the likes of the guns Sheriff Connell's been tellin' us about is goin' to be a whole lot of a one-sided affair to my thinkin',' voiced a straw-chewing man shielding his eyes against the glare. 'And I ain't certain as how that's for Bandyrock.'

There were more murmurs of understanding and approval.

A stouter, red-faced fellow stepped forward.

'Too right it ain't for Bandyrock,' he offered. 'We're peace-lovin' folk doin' our best to settle a territory – but so was Jake Wardman. Hell, him and Martha had been scratchin' out that spread of theirs for the best part of their lives. From what the sheriff says, they didn't have no choice at all. Not a spit of one.'

'And what about young Jessie,' added the man at his side. 'What the hell are them scumbags doin' with her – as if we can't guess – and supposin' Jake's along of her seein' it all, what in the name of sanity must he be thinkin' and feelin'? Fella must be clean out of his head by now. No wife, no home, no hogs, no spread and his daughter in the hands of vermin. Can't just turn our backs on him, can we? Too darned right we can't!'

The straw-chewing man slid the stalk across his mouth as he thrust his hands into his pockets.

'I ain't sayin' as how I'm against doin' the best we can for Jake and Jessie, but, hell, I ain't fired a piece in years.'

'That goes for most of us,' called a man from the back of the gathering.

The blacksmith thrust the folds of his rolled shirt-sleeves to the top of his arms and stiffened his shoulders.

'Just have to learn to handle a gun again, won't

you?' He glared at the faces watching him. 'This ain't no debatin' matter. Can't be, not where there's murder and kidnappin' involved, and especially not when it's folk as close as the Wardmans. Damn it, they were as good as kin.'

'No denyin' that,' supported the storekeeper.

'You've all heard what the sheriff found out there at the spread – he didn't mince his words none,' continued Levens, folding his arms. 'Frank Connell will do all he can by us, I know that, you know that. Mebbe we'll raise help out of Morristown or Gentry. But mebbe we won't, so we've got to be ready right here, right now, just in case them scumbags are plannin' on a visit.'

'And while we're waitin',' asked Doc, 'what do we do about Jake and Jessie?'

'We go talk to the sheriff, get him to agree to a dozen of us ridin' out before sundown.'

'Ridin' out to where, to do what exactly?'

'To scour the Bluespeck Hills. . . .'

SIX

'You can't let 'em do it, Frank. You're goin' to have to stop 'em.' Doc Merry paced the length of the Split Spurs saloon to the batwings, turned and stared like an angry hawk at Sheriff Connell.

'Don't see how, short of lockin' up half the town.' Connell came slowly to his feet at the corner table and crossed quietly through the shadowy gloom of the deserted bar to Doc's side. 'I know how they feel, mebbe more so – I was out there. I buried Martha.'

'Ain't nobody doubtin' what you saw and what you did, Frank, and I'd reckon for the whole town bein' aware of what Quantril and his rats are likely to threaten, but, hell, that's one thing; men ridin' out to scour the Bluespecks is another.' Doc's eyes darkened. 'Where would they begin? How long would they search: a day, two, three, a week? And just supposin' they did meet up with Quantril; found Jake and Jessie alive. What then?' He paused to swallow. 'Raw guns Bandyrock style ain't no match for the likes of murderin', lootin' scumbags. You know that as well as I do.'

'I know it,' said the sheriff, 'but right now . . .'

Both men eased through the batwings at the sound of running steps pounding down the boardwalk.

'Sure glad I've found you, Mr Connell,' gasped a short, twitchy-faced fellow, sweating to a halt at the 'wings. 'Thought you should know, Adam Levens and Cord Chappel have just ridden out. Said as how they were plannin' on scourin' for Jake and Jessie. Figured as how they might pick up a trail before nightfall.' The man gulped. 'What you reckon, Mr Connell?'

Quantril and his men, with Jake and Jessie roped to trail mounts taken from the Wardman spread, had travelled on a long, twisting route on their way to the outskirts of Bandyrock, Prof Markham insisting on using all the remote tracks he could deduce from the parchment map.

'I ain't for us doin' anythin' obvious for others to seize on,' he had ordered to the scowling faces of Stock and McCane and the uncaring stare of Charlie Loome. 'What we got here with the old man and the girl is too valuable to get to treatin' it lightly. Squander either one of 'em and we're the losers – which is why we come up on Bandyrock like wolves who ain't eaten for days and are relishin' the meal to come. Understand? You follow me?'

'Good thinkin', Prof,' Quantril had agreed. 'We do as you say, don't we, boys?'

'Till when?' Stock had sneered.

'Till I say other.' Prof had grinned. 'And that, judgin' by the light and the state of the track we're followin', will be some time coming. So let's move, eh?'

The sun was down and the early evening shadows were already thickening when Prof signalled for the line of riders to halt in a clearing among thickets of scrub, tumbled rocks and a scattering of full-grown pines.

'No fire,' he announced, still mounted. 'We eat cold and stay with our canteens. Somebody look to the girl and her pa. And no messin'. We stay quiet and keep it easy. You take first watch, Charlie.'

The party had settled within the hour, Quantril watchful through the deepening darkness, aware of every movement made, aware of even the slightest sound that might have seemed out of place, the softest murmurings among the men.

Prof dozed peacefully beneath the tilted derby. Stock and McCane rested with their backs to the pines, their gazes flitting like night moths from Quantril, along the line of loose-hitched mounts to the old man roped once again to a tree, his daughter silent, shivering and bewildered at his feet.

'Know somethin', Rimms,' Stock had eventually said, 'I have a fancy for a whole night in a real feather bed, with real pillows and smooth sheets and mebbe that young gal along of me. You figure I might get lucky when we reach this two-bit town we're headin' for?'

'You might, but I wouldn't bank on it,' shrugged McCane. 'Quantril and Prof ain't much for partyin' right now, specially where that filly's concerned. 'Sides, I ain't never slept in no feather bed with all them trimmin's, so I wouldn't know.'

'But you've got a hankerin' for the gal, eh?' Stock

smiled. 'You ain't denyin' that. We ain't goin' to let her slip through our fingers, are we? Prof ain't havin' everythin' his own way.'

McCane shifted uncomfortably.

'Best watch that tongue of yours, fella. Get you into a heap of trouble if you ain't careful. I wouldn't be for meddlin' with Quantril's mood at the moment.'

Stock spat deliberately beyond his outstretched legs.

'So?' he grunted, 'So whose life is this, anyhow? And what's so big about that southern border?'

'I'll tell you what's big about it,' hissed McCane. 'If we don't cross it like Prof says with dollars in our pockets, we ain't goin' to be lookin' to nothin' save the bone yard, and that's for a fact. So shut your eyes to the gal out there and your mouth along of 'em and get some sleep.'

Charlie Loome had watched the night close in and the full moon rise as if watching a first coat of black paint being brushed across a canvas. There had been no movement out there in the sprawling mass of the Bluespeck Hills – leastways none that he had detected – and no sounds save for the occasional call of a bird, hoot of an owl, the padding through scrub of a prowling animal.

Now, as the darkness lengthened and thickened, the moon stared, the shadows lay like sleeping limbs, all, he might have thought, was as it should be.

But it was not.

There could be up to a dozen guns out there; guns that had trailed them patiently, diligently since Morristown and Gentry. Guns that were anxious for retribution wherever, whenever the opportunity came.

And there might be one gun much closer.

Charlie had positioned himself a matter of only a few yards from Jake Wardman and his daughter. He had them in his sight through the shadows and was within earshot of their murmurings and whispers as the night had settled.

'You hold on in there, gal,' Jake had croaked, straining instinctively against the ropes binding him. 'You hear me, Jessie?'

The girl's response had been no more than a sob against the fear in her head and the pain that throbbed through the rope wound tight at her wrists.

'Goddamnit . . .' the old man had moaned. 'One of these days somebody is sure as hell's fire goin' to pay for this. I swear that on the memory of your ma. So you just do as she'd have wanted of you, Jessie: you just keep right on breathin' and fightin' and believin' . . . We ain't done yet, not by a long shot we ain't.'

Jake had strained again, licked the cold sweat from his lips and blinked aside the welling emotion in his tired eyes. 'You bet we ain't done,' he had murmured in a voice that had seemed to come from somewhere behind steam. 'I just got this gut feelin' that Sheriff Connell might get to. . . . Hell, I love you, gal. I love you . . . .'

It was mention of the name Connell that had raised the prickle in Charlie Loome's neck.

The name had taken him back instantly to another place, another time; images of a street, a shoot-out, bodies, guns, the voices of the law.

Had the name Connell been among those he had

heard all that long time ago? Was the same fellow here now? A sheriff? The law at Bandyrock? Maybe he should go question the old man closer, get him to tell . . . .

And then Charlie had heard the sound. Not the call of a bird or the prowl of an animal.

The steps of a man.

SEVEN

'Easy, easy,' hissed the voice. Adam Levens tightened his grip on Cord Chappel's arm and halted him in the depths of the scrub and rocks. He listened, watched, swallowed. 'We ain't alone,' he hissed again, his eyes flashing on the moonlight. He tensed. 'Move over to the left there, and keep it real soft.'

Cord nodded and eased away on slow, careful steps, the blacksmith following like a shadow.

They had progressed no more than a dozen yards to within the cover of low slung pine branches, when Adam urged a halt.

'This don't feel right,' he whispered. 'Mebbe we should back off 'til first light. If there's somebody about, we ain't doin' no good makin' all this noise.'

'We ain't makin' no noise,' murmured Cord, 'and I ain't spooked none about not bein' alone. Mebbe we're gettin' close. Could be we've run into them murderin' scumbags.'

'But not in the dark,' persisted Adam. 'It's too dangerous. I say we leave it. Settle for a couple of hours, then take another look.'

'Agreed,' said Cord, 'but not before we're through these pines. We'll take cover in rocks. It'll be safer.'

They crept on, creaking and snapping their way over a carpet of loose scrub, scattered twigs and fallen cones, Adam increasingly uncertain of the hasty decision to leave town with only Chappel in the search for Jake and Jessie. Maybe they should have waited, recruited more men, ridden out at first light instead of the fading end of the day. More important, he should have discussed the decision a whole lot closer with Sheriff Connell.

Deep anger and blood-racing concern for the fate of Jake and Jessie were understandable, even to be commended, but trailing out here in the foothills of the Bluespecks in the dark, on unknown territory, with the horses hitched some way back, a murdering gun likely at the next turn, might be seen as downright irresponsible.

'Hell!' cursed Adam through his teeth at the snagging grip of a twist of scrub. He paused a moment to free his pants from the fingering burrs, blink and adjust his focus again on the patchwork of shadows and looming shapes surrounding him, and try to pinpoint just how far ahead Cord had moved.

'You there?' he hissed, not daring now to take another step until he had Chappel in his sight. 'Cord – you still here?'

Silence. Nothing save the sound of his own breathing, the murmur of soft scrub as he shifted a foot. He hissed another call, waited, screwed his eyes to a new focus, began to sweat. If Cord had taken matters into his own hands, he began to reason as he eased on, then this time there would be no arguing; they would be turning back, heading down the main trail to Bandyrock, and they would be riding like the wind, no stopping till they reached town.

The gunshot cracked across the night as if ripping it apart.

A bird clattered high above the pines. An animal scurried into hidden depths. A girl screamed, a man moaned, and Adam Levens froze where he stood.

'Cord?' he murmured, knowing instinctively that there would be no answer. He dropped lower, sweating freely in spite of the night chill. Should he go on? What had Cord seen? More important, who had seen Cord?

He backed slowly, carefully, reaching the pines again as softly as a shadow. Maybe he should wait, establish just what had happened.

But, damn it, he already knew! Cord had come just a step too close to whoever of Quantril's men had been posted look-out, and there had been no hesitation from the gunslinger. He had probably shot as much on sound as he had on a sighting.

Adam took a deep breath, wiped a hand over his sweat-soaked face, blinked and stiffened at the sudden clamour of voices only yards away.

'What the hell's goin' on?'

'Who've you shot, Charlie? You know the rat?'

'Never seen him before.'

'He out of Bandyrock?'

'Got to be if we're this close.'

'Hell, that means they mebbe know we're comin'.'

'Never mind what they may or may not know. 'T'ain't of no consequence right now. What about the old man and the girl? They safe enough?'

'Safe and tight as ever.'

'Good. Then somebody go take a look to see if our visitor came alone. And if there's anybody out there, kill 'em, whoever they are.'

It took the blacksmith only seconds to make up his mind what to do next. He backed a half-dozen carefully measured steps, paused, licked the sweat from his lips, turned and made off in a straight line for the hitched horses.

He was riding out of the foothills within minutes.

'So the old man recognizes him?' said Prof, pacing through the shadows to Quantril's side.

'Reckons so. Says his name's Cord Chappel, long-time helpin' hand to Bandyrock's blacksmith.'

'Sonofabitch,' cursed McCane, slapping a fist to the palm of his hand. 'I figured all along somethin' like this would happen. Just knew it, minute we set foot in these miserable hills.' He spat fiercely and glared at Prof. 'You know what this means, don't you? You've figured it – 'cus if you ain't, I sure as hell have!'

'Brilliant,' grinned Prof. 'I wouldn't have thought you had it in you. So, please, Mr McCane, do enlighten us.'

Quantril shifted impatiently. Jason Stock sniggered. Charlie Loome frowned, still pondering on the name the old man had mentioned.

'That dead body back there means only one thing – Bandyrock's waitin' on us. Every last man. And if they

40

ain't waitin', they'll soon be ridin'. Dozens of 'em, swarmin' over these hills like ants at a honeypot. Somebody, somehow, got on to us. They know all about the old man and the gal. Damn it, they could have ridden out to that homestead and found the dead woman. And for all we know they could be raisin' posses from here to the border. Hell, there's mebbe anythin' close on a hundred men out there waitin' on us.'

'You all through?' said Prof as McCane continued to glare like a petrified jack rabbit. 'That's quite a catalogue of possibilities you got there, young fella. Your brain's been workin' round the clock, though it seems to have rattled clear of the only thing that counts.' Prof fell silent for a moment. 'You know what I'm talkin' about, Mr McCane?'

'I ain't botherin'—' began McCane.

'Put it this way,' continued Prof majestically, 'when I'm sittin' at the gamblin' table cradlin' a flush hand, I ain't fussed none how long it takes for the others to shuffle and rearrange their hands. They can take all the time in the world. I ain't worried because I *know* the hand I'm holdin' is the only one that can win.' He grinned again and adjusted his bandanna. 'We, Mr McCane, have the old man and his daughter. A winning hand if ever I saw one.'

'You're settin' an awful lot by that gal and her pa,' growled McCane. 'Supposin'—'

'Supposin' the folk of Bandyrock don't buy it,' sneered Stock, lumping his weight to one hip. 'Supposin' they're them kinda folk: mean and cold and hard-bitten as stale jerky.' He nodded his head as

41

if to agree with himself. 'Supposin',' he began again slowly, 'they had no neighbourin' with the family out there at the homestead. Just supposin' *that*.'

'About as likely as hogs sproutin' wings,' growled Quantril, scratching at his thickening stubble. 'I'm with Prof on this one. We're holdin' a winnin' hand here. But right now, we're wastin' good time again. We should be edgin' closer to Bandyrock.'

'Or,' cautioned Prof, 'askin' ourselves if the fella Charlie's just so efficiently silenced was out here alone. Perhaps he had a companion. I personally find it unlikely that he was a lone rider. What do you reckon, Charlie?'

Loome ran a hand over his gut.

'Saw and heard only one – and he's dead.' He spat. 'You want I should go over the body?'

'I lay claim to his boots,' snapped Stock. 'I ain't had a decent pair of boots in years.'

Prof adjusted his derby to a jaunty angle.

'Do with the body as you please. Meantime, we'll have first light in under two hours. Let's be ready to ride soon as we can see the track. Destination by noon: Bandyrock!'

Charlie Loome decided he would say nothing for now of who might be wearing the law badge when they rode in.

EIGHT

'Too late. We've left it too late. They'll be here come midday and then all hell will break loose.' The tall, angular man with a limp made his way to the batwings of the Split Spurs saloon, gazed into the early morning light and stifled a shiver. 'I lived here in Bandyrock all my workin' life. Raised the family here. Never thought I'd come to see this day.'

Sheriff Connell cleared his throat and turned to address the gathering of town men. 'I ain't for talk like Eli's puttin' it there. We might be late in comin' to this situation, but I don't believe we're too late.'

'So what you sayin', Sheriff?' asked Bernard Wheeler, tugging at his frock-coat. 'You figured on some way out of this?'

'No, that I haven't. Nor is there one. We must face whatever's comin' to us. We owe that much to the memory of Cord and for the sake of Jake and Jessie. They ain't dead – not yet – that much we do know. And they're alive for a purpose. Luke Quantril ain't no charitable institution. If he's keepin' Jake and the gal breathin', he's got a price he's lookin' to collect.

43

And that, by my reckonin', is goin' to be right here in Bandyrock.'

The town men shifted uncomfortably and murmured among themselves. Sheriff Connell waited, glancing quickly from Wheeler to Doc Merry, then to the man at the door.

'A blood-bath here in the street?' said Eli. 'Is that what we're lookin' to?'

Adam Levens pushed back his chair and came unsteadily to his feet, the trail dust from the ride out of the hills still flaking from his clothes.

'Tell you somethin',' he croaked, 'them scumbags out there don't waste no breath debatin' the issue.' He wiped a lathering of cold sweat and grime from his brow and stared vacantly into the faces watching him. 'I should've stayed,' he croaked again. 'Should've been with Cord when he needed me. Damn it, I should never have let him go on like that. What in the name of sanity was I thinkin' of, f'cris'sake?' His voice cracked, faltered and petered away.

'Easy there, fella, easy,' soothed Doc Merry, hurrying to the blacksmith's side. 'You need to rest a while. Time to catch up on some sleep, eh?'

The saloon bar gathering watched in silence as Doc led Adam away through the shadows to the batwings.

'Had a bad time back there,' piped a bushy-bearded fellow, lighting his pipe anxiously.

'Cord was hard-workin' and God-fearin'. One of the best,' echoed a man at the back of the room.

'And he might be the first of many,' called another. 'Mebbe the whole darned lot of us will go the same way.'

44

'Hold it right there,' shouted Wheeler above the sudden babble of voices, scraping of chairs and boots, clink of bottles to glasses. 'That's just fool talk and it ain't goin' to get us nowhere. So let's cut it out, shall we?'

'Can't stick your head in the sand and hope that types like Quantril and his rats'll go away,' said Eli, limping back to the bar. He blew into his cupped hands against the chill that had seeped through the 'wings. 'I ain't condonin' what Cord and Adam did. Hot-headed if you ask me, but, hell, they meant well, did what they reckoned was the right thing. And there ain't no condemnin' a man for that. But we've all heard clear as day what Adam experienced out there. Make no mistake, that scream he heard came from Jessie. No doubtin' about that. And I ain't doubtin' that Quantril's headin' this way, just like the sheriff says. Question now, Mr Wheeler, is what do we do?'

Eli glanced at the clock on the wall. 'We've got about five hours by my reckonin'.'

Doc Merry hurried from the livery where he had settled Adam Levens into a deep sleep and crossed the now sunlit main street to Sheriff Connell's office.

He paused briefly on the boardwalk to glance along the line of silent deserted buildings. No sign of activity at Wheeler's mercantile, no customers at the barber's shop; the timber yard stood without a movement among the planks and poles and fencing. No visitors at Ma Pretty's clothing store, and even the funeral parlour seemed blacker in the mood of tense waiting. Only the potman at the Split Spurs saloon,

45

under the watchful eye of proprietor Jay Matlan and a clutch of bar girls at the windows, went about his daily business of sweeping the boardwalk, but without the enthusiastic swish and swirl of the ancient besom. Bandyrock was sweating and shivering at the same time.

Doc hurried on again, this time without pausing, to reach the sheriff's office, open the door and step inside.

'Dead as Boot Hill out there,' he grunted, brushing the dust from his jacket. 'Spooky.' He stared carefully at Connell for a moment before adding; 'What's the plan? We got one?'

Sheriff Connell turned from his gun cabinet, a polished Winchester gleaming in his grip. 'As many men as I can muster posted look-out round the town. Strictly no shootin' is the order. If we're goin' to get anywhere with Quantril and, more important, that schemin' sidekick, Prof Markham, we're goin' to have to talk. Flyin' lead will end in only one thing, a blood-bath. Quantril's thinkin' don't usually extend much above dead bodies. So we keep it steady, stay calm and just trust we can get him out of here with the town still in one piece.'

Doc nodded. 'You can count on me. And that goes for the rest of us. Meantime, what's the chances of help from Morristown or Gentry?'

'Slim,' said Connell. 'Too late to send a rider out, and I can't spare a man anyhow. But I ain't ruled out the possibility of a posse closin' in from some place.' He crossed to the window overlooking the deserted street. 'For now, we can only wait.'

*

Jay Matlan spun round in a cloud of cigar smoke and stared at the woman seated on the bed. 'Are you sure, absolutely sure?' A drift of ash cascaded across his fancy waistcoat. 'It was some time back. You could be mistaken.'

The girl, somewhere in her late twenties, fair-haired, good-looking and known affectionately around Bandyrock and more particularly to the customers at the Split Spurs simply as Abigail, crossed her legs petulantly and cupped a knee in her hands.

'You don't meet up with the likes of Luke Quantril and forget it,' she said, her stare matter-of-fact and unblinking. 'I ain't one jot mistaken. I met up with Quantril four years back in Dubarry out Kansas way. I can still feel the bruisin'.'

Matlan sucked nervously at the cigar, let the smoke swirl for a moment, then paced deliberately back to the window. 'Supposin' he recognizes you?'

'Oh, he'll recognize me, sure enough. Don't you fret on that. Quantril don't forget nothin', and even when he does there's always that deadly rattler, Prof, slitherin' at his heels.'

'So you'd best stay out of sight 'til all this is over,' said Matlan, turning again to face the girl.

'The hell I will!' snapped Abigail, the colour flaring in her cheeks. 'I'm mebbe goin' to be the only one round here with any edge on the rat. No, I ain't hidin' myself away, not nohow I ain't. You get yourself over to Sheriff Connell right now. Tell him as the town's got itself the best go-between it's ever likely to have. And

47

you can take it from me, Jay Matlan, I'll do all I can for a payback on Luke Quantril, and 'specially seein' as how he's holdin' that young Jessie Wardman. God knows what scumbag hands have been pawin' over her.'

Abigail uncrossed her legs, stood up and smoothed her hands down the folds of her dress. 'Now just scoot, will you? I got things to do which ain't for your eyes.'

NINE

The last hour to noon on that hot, sunlit day was the longest ever known in Bandyrock. Sheriff Connell watched the hands of the clock on the wall in his office tick on minute by minute to midday as if watching the beat of his own heart.

Doc Merry stood silent and lost in his own thoughts at the window, conscious of the street beyond the dusty panes, yet sometimes not seeing it or the lengthening shadows.

Bernard Wheeler closed the store early, ensured that some of his more expensive wares were removed to the back room, and unlocked his personal gun cabinet for the first time in years. He strapped on a silver-buckled gun belt with tooled leather holster, selected a bone-handled Colt from his collection and felt, for that moment anyhow, a whole lot safer. He had been reluctant to admit that he had not held a gun or fired a shot in more than a year.

Jay Matlan had hurried from the Split Spurs saloon to the sheriff's office to report Abigail's news and pass on her message without once pausing to dust the cigar ash from his waistcoat. He could sense trouble, big trouble that would almost certainly see his saloon damaged, if not destroyed, his liquor stocks depleted to a dribble, and his bar girls abused. He figured it an odds-on wager that Abigail would get herself killed and he would finish up bankrupted beyond salvation.

His message delivered, he had left Sheriff Connell and Doc Merry to debate its implications. He had other matters to reckon with on what he had already concluded was just a sad, bad day.

Adam Levens had slept fitfully in a lathering of sweat and a haunting of images. He had witnessed the death of his good friend Cord more than a dozen times in his dreams, heard the shots, the screams, the echoing voices of Quantril and his men; seen himself riding clear of the Bluespecks until, like some ghostly spectre, he had disappeared in a blaze of light.

He had finally woken, doused himself under the hand pump back of the stabling, cooked a thick steak on the forge, eaten it along of strong black coffee, consulted his timepiece and been well satisfied to note that there was still a whole ten minutes to pass until noon.

Only then had he taken the time to carefully check out his Colt.

Eli had limped his way to the welcome shade on the boardwalk fronting the Split Spurs and settled himself in the chair to the left of the 'wings. He could see darn near the length of the street from here, clear away to the Bluespecks to the north, petering away to the lonely desert trail to the south.

Town was quiet now, he thought, running a hand

over his stubble. Quieter than it had ever been on any summer's day that he could recall. Never figured he would see it, but it was a scared quietness, a silence that stifled and smothered Bandyrock in a cloak of its own fear.

But there were eyes about. Sure there were: three look-outs posted at the north end of the street; eyes at windows, men, women, youngsters. Eyes just about everywhere when you came to reckon it. And all of them waiting on Quantril and his men.

It was exactly noon when they rode in.

They came at an easy pace on a gentle scuff of hoofs, slow jangle of tack and creak of leather. Luke Quantril rode at their head, Prof to his right, Charlie Loome to the left. Jason Stock and Rimms McCane brought up the rear, Stock trailing Jake Wardman, McCane his daughter. They reached the top of the street, the Bluespecks shimmering behind them, and reined up on Quantril's signal. Then they simply sat and stared and waited, their shadows sprawling before them, the mounts tossing heads, flicking tails against the noonday flies. The silence in those moments lay as thick as the heat.

'Hell, look at the state of that poor gal,' murmured Doc Merry as he followed Sheriff Connell from the office to the boardwalk. 'She needs attention, and soon.'

'All in good time, Doc,' soothed Connell, his gaze narrowing on the group of men. He settled his grip on the Winchester held loose at his side and took a first step to the street. 'Walk with me, but not too close, and don't look around you.'

'You got men posted nearby?' asked Doc.

'Rooftops. But they've got their orders.'

Doc swallowed deeply and fell into step behind the sheriff. 'Hell,' he murmured again, his eyes squinting on the glare.

Connell slowed and eventually halted some twenty yards short of the mounted men. He let the weapon stay loose at his side, his only movement being to tip his hat to deepen the shade across his gaze. 'Name's Connell,' he said. 'Sheriff hereabouts.' His eyes flicked to Jake and Jessie. 'Seems like we got some talkin' to do.'

Quantril spat and stared. Prof fingered his bandanna. Charlie Loome's frown deepened in his concentration on Connell's face. McCane and Stock grinned. The old man and his daughter sat in silence, their eyes working frantically from Doc and the sheriff to the familiar street, the buildings, the very dirt and dust of the place that lifted their hearts if not their hopes.

Doc took an impatient step forward, the sweat on his face glistening like raindrops. 'Ain't a darn thing we can do about the carnage you fellas have left behind you,' he flared under Connell's restraining hand, 'and don't think we don't know about Jake's wife and the murderin' destruction you wreaked back there at his place – Sheriff Connell's seen it all for himself. And we know you killed Cord Chappel. Some tally you got there, not to mention who's come before. But speakin' as the doc in these parts, I'm tellin' you that girl you got there needs attention right now.

52

Same goes for her pa. Furthermore—'

'You ain't tellin' me nothin', mister.' Quantril glowered and gave an angry flick of the reins. 'I'm doin' the tellin' round here, and if you've got any sense you'll be listenin' up real close.'

Connell urged Doc Merry to hold his tongue and simmer down. Loome's concentration on the sheriff had not wandered. Stock pushed his hat clear of the sweaty tightness across his brow. McCane wiped his mouth.

It was Prof who, at last, cleared his throat importantly. 'Perhaps I'll do the tellin', shall I?' He grinned. 'There's nothin' too difficult about it.' He adjusted the derby with a primed hand. 'As you see, Sheriff, we are holdin' both the girl and her father. They're doubtless somewhat exhausted, maybe a touch confused and, naturally, a mite sorrowful bearin' in mind the unfortunate circumstances surroundin' their capture. However—'

Doc pulled himself clear of the sheriff's hold on his arm. 'Get to it, fella! All that fancy spoutin' don't impress me none. Hell, we know who you are, what you stand for and the scumbag reputations you're draggin' along of you, *And* we know all about Morristown and Gentry. You bet. Fact is, there's every chance of a posse sittin' on your tails right now. You can bet to that too.'

'Talkative, ain't he?' sneered Stock. 'You want I should puncture that windpipe, Mr Quantril?'

Quantril smiled and spat again. McCane tipped his hat lazily and chewed on a fresh plug of tobacco. Loome continued to concentrate on Sheriff Connell, who had at last managed to cool Doc's anger.

'As I was sayin',' said Prof with little more than a glance at the florid faced doctor, 'the girl and the old man are, shall we say, distressed, but they are alive. And that, Sheriff Connell, is a blessin', don't you think?' He ran his fingers through the bandanna for a moment, then settled his gaze in an ice-cold stare. 'So here's the deal.'

Connell tensed, conscious of Doc's muttered curse, the glare and shimmer of the light, the dry, burning air. Somewhere a dog yapped and was silenced instantly; a window slid closed as if taking a last breath. Eli got to his feet from the chair on the boardwalk and eased back through the shade to the batwings where Jay Matlan waited, an unlit cigar cushioned between his stubby fingers. A bar girl behind him sniffed loudly. Abigail moved softly to a window and stifled a shiver at the sight, even at this distance, of Luke Quantril.

'Our only interest is in getting clear of here to the southern border,' Prof continued, his stare deepening to a brooding darkness. 'And for that, and our future, we need money. All we can get. Every last dollar. And Bandyrock is goin' to provide it.'

'Like hell it is!' flared Doc, scuffing dirt under his boots as Connell's grip restrained him.

'We shall see.' Prof grinned, his gaze settling on Connell. 'You, Sheriff, will ensure that every business in this town, every homestead, every pocket of everybody is emptied of every dollar it has and is delivered to me. Failure to do so will result in only one thing. . . . Simply put and without my spellin' out all the gory details of the actual doin', the old man and the girl will die. The girl, of course, being the last to go.'

Prof's glare brightened under the shimmering noon heat. 'You have, Sheriff Connell, only hours.'

TEN

Eli limped through the afternoon shadows along the alley at the side of the Split Spurs saloon, waited when he reached the clutter of empty barrels, crates and boxes, then hissed through the gap in his front teeth. Ten seconds later his close friend and neighbour, Harry Macks, slid like a snake to Eli's side and blinked nervously through a swamp of dusty sweat.

'I ain't so sure about this,' muttered Harry, wiping his face. 'Takin' one helluva risk, aren't we? I mean, I ain't never tangled with types like them before, and I ain't sure that now's the time to start.'

Eli drew Harry deeper into the shadows behind a pile of crates. 'Nothin' to it. All we're goin' to do is take a peek. If we can find out just where them rats are holdin' Jake and Jessie, then mebbe we'll have a real chance when it comes to stormin' the place.'

Harry's face bloomed under a new rush of sweat. 'Storm the place – hell, we goin' to do that?'

'Sheriff Connell and the others ain't goin' to take all this lyin' down, are they? I'll say not. So it behoves us all to do what we can. Every little's goin' to help, otherwise that Quantril fella's goin' to strip this town 'til it hurts, and there ain't goin' to be no sayin' as to how many bodies will pile up – includin', remember, that poor gal in there. So let's get busy, eh?'

'What's your plan?'

'I got a notion that Matlan don't always get to lockin' that back door there 'til after dark. If I can get through there, I figure on gettin' a view of the bar, see what's really goin' on. We've got to know how Quantril's distributin' his men now that he seems to have settled himself and his scum in the saloon. But I need eyes at the back of me, watchin' to see all's clear. That's where you come in, Harry. You're goin' to be my eyes.'

Eli tensed at the sound of glass shattering somewhere deep in the bar. 'Cover me,' he murmured, and limped out of the shadow like an anxious crab.

'What's happenin'? They makin' any move?' Doc Merry moved along the boardwalk facing the Split Spurs until he reached the deepest shadow at the mercantile's window. He narrowed his gaze, then spoke in a hushed mutter to the man at his side. 'What you reckon, Bernard, them sonsofbitches settlin' in?'

'With a vengeance,' said the storekeeper, gripping the lapels of his coat. 'Won't be nothin' left of the place time they're all through. As for the folk in there – Jake and Jessie, Abigail and the girls, Matlan, the potman . . . Hell, I wouldn't be where they are for all the money in the world.'

'And speakin' of money—' began Doc again.

'We ain't got no choice. We're goin' to have to do

precisely as Quantril wants: collect as much cash as we can, or can get away with and hand it over. That way we stay breathin'.'

'Sonofa-goddamn-bitch,' mouthed Doc, squinting again into the glare in the street. 'Sheriff goin' along with that?' he asked.

'Again, no choice, has he? There's just too much at stake to do anythin' else.'

'Damn it, we can't sit back and let all this just happen. 'T'ain't right. We owe it to ourselves to do *somethin'*. Jake would say the same, I know he would.'

Wheeler grunted and rolled his shoulders. 'But Jake'll know well enough the dilemma we're facin'. Damned if we do and damned if we don't.'

'Abigail says she knows Quantril from way back. Mebbe she'll be able to help.'

'Don't see how,' said Wheeler. 'Them rats in there are pretty desperate. They're on the run with only one way to head: due south to the border. There ain't nothin' goin' to put 'em off achievin' that.' He rolled his shoulders again. 'But at the same time they're smart, especially that one they call Prof. Strikes me he's the outfit's brains. He knows there ain't no future stiflin' in Mexican heat and dust with a pocketful of nothin'.'

'I see that, but all the same . . .'

Doc halted mid flow as the batwings at the Split Spurs swung open and Quantril, with Rimms McCane toting a Colt in each hand, pushed Eli and Harry Macks across the boardwalk.

'Connell,' shouted Quantril, his right boot crunching Eli's arm to the boards, 'this one of your crazy notions? You figurin' on delayin' us or somethin'? Caught these two skulkin' about back of the bar. Now that ain't playin' the game, is it? You want this should get dirty?'

The sheriff had left his office and reached the street at the first crack of Quantril's voice. Now, his body tensed, fists clenched at his side, he glared without blinking at Quantril and McCane. But there was no hiding his fury at the townsmen's actions.

'Sheriff looks fit to burst a blood-vessel,' murmured Doc from the shadows.

'What the hell does Eli think he's doin'?' said the storekeeper, pulling nervously at his coat lapels. 'He tryin' to get himself killed or somethin'?'

'Mebbe figured he was helpin' somehow,' answered Doc.

Connell took another careful step into the full shimmering heat of the street. 'They ain't under my orders,' he called, his stare tight on Quantril. 'But you can let 'em go. You've got my word it won't happen again.'

'Too damned right it won't,' snapped Quantril. 'You've got more important matters to be lookin' to – like collectin' that money together. We're patient men, Sheriff, but we got our limits. You readin' me?'

'I'm readin' you. I understand,' said Connell. 'Meantime, you release those men.'

Quantril's eyes were unmoving for a moment, fixed like lights on the sheriff's face. He spat deliberately into the dirt ahead of him, muttered something to McCane then slowly eased his boot from Eli's arm.

McCane shoved Harry Macks to the street. Eli

followed on his shuffling limp. Quantril folded his arms. Sheriff Connell watched the townsmen's steps as if counting and measuring them.

'He's lettin' 'em go,' murmured Doc Merry, blinking quickly on a surge of sweat.

Bernard Wheeler rolled his shoulders and swallowed noisily.

Connell continued to count. Five, six, seven . . . The two men had reached the middle of the street when McCane spun the Colt in his left hand and holstered it with a decisive thud.

A trickle of cold sweat inched into the sheriff's neck as his gaze narrowed, his mouth dried and fists tightened until the knuckles gleamed white.

'No!' he croaked in the sudden realization of what was about to happen, the sound of his voice already lost in the spitting blaze of McCane's second Colt. The three fast shots spun Harry Macks like a top, arched his body, spun him again, then threw him back to the baking dirt as if no more than something discarded on a sudden wind.

Eli fell to his knees where he stood. Connell groaned, his limbs as leaden as weights. Doc Merry blinked, sweated, swallowed and seemed for a while to be melting as Wheeler's hand fell across his arm like something wet and limp.

'Let that be a lesson, Connell,' growled Quantril across the heat haze. 'Mark it, but don't be fooled – next time nobody gets spared.' He spat furiously. 'Now get that mess off the street and then get busy.'

ELEVEN

Doc Merry slid his fingers down the jar of colourfully striped candy and rested them a moment on the polished counter before turning his gaze on the faces of the others gathered in the lantern-lit gloom of Wheeler's mercantile.

'If it's any consolation,' he said quietly, 'Harry would've died on the first shot. He wouldn't have known a thing after that.'

A grey-faced man standing at the side of a pile of blankets grunted his understanding. 'Suppose that's somethin',' he murmured. 'Harry Macks didn't deserve to die sufferin'. What about Eli?'

Doc gave the jar one last tap and stepped clear of the counter. 'Eli's keepin' himself to himself right now. Feels the need. Can't say I blame him.'

'Darn fool thing he did back there,' said a towns-man, wiping his brow with a bandanna. 'What the hell did he think he was doin' against types like Quantril?'

'He was doin' what a lot of us are thinkin', only he had the guts to try,' said Doc bluntly. 'Foolish? Mebbe. A wasted life? Certainly. Cord Chappel was another.

Martha Wardman had no choice.'

'So who's next?' asked a man at the back of the store. 'And where do we go from here?'

'I'll tell you where we don't go,' said Sheriff Connell, easing himself clear of the sacks of flour and beans. 'There'll be no more single-handed attempts against Quantril. Nobody does a thing without my say-so.'

'And I'm backin' that,' said Wheeler. 'We can't afford any more deaths. We're sittin' on enough trouble as it is. No point in addin' to it.'

'You sayin' as how we sit back and do nothin'?' snapped Adam Levens, pushing at his rolled shirt-sleeves.

'No, I ain't sayin' that exactly,' explained Wheeler. 'All I'm sayin' is—'

'If we do nothin', there'll be nothin' left, and that's the size of it,' pronounced a clean-shaven youth with wide blue eyes.

The blacksmith pushed at his sleeves again. 'He's got a point there. Figure it so far: we know to the dead – nothin' we can do about them, pool souls – and we know to them under direct threat and where they are. They're across the street, right there at the Split Spurs, and so are Quantril's scum.' He folded his arms dramatically. 'What say we plan an all-out attack? Spring it on 'em a few hours before dawn. What you reckon?'

The men talked and murmured and shifted among themselves. Bernard Wheeler sighed and shook his head. Sheriff Connell crossed to the store's glass door and gazed into the dark, shadow-filled street where only the lights from the saloon bore a sign of any life.

Doc Merry tapped on the counter for attention and waited patiently for the gathering to fall silent. 'I'll tell you straight up,' he began. 'I ain't much for scrapin' up dead bodies. I've always done the best I know how by the sick, the injured and the infirm, but when it comes to a shoot-out between us and Quantril, I gotta tell you we'd be creatin' a blood-bath. No sayin' as to how many dead I'd be cartin' out of the dirt.'

He raised a hand to quieten the murmurings. 'That said, I ain't for doin' nothin'. Nossir, I ain't for that. But we gotta think of somethin' a whole lot smarter than blazin' lead from part-time guns. So let's get busy, eh? Let's think. . . .'

Abigail dismissed Luke Quantril's devouring stare with a toss of her head and flick of her hair and crossed the smoke-hazed bar to the cooler, fresher night at the batwings.

'Dubarry,' was all he had said on first setting eyes on her on his arrival in Bandyrock. 'Yeah, Dubarry. I remember that. You recall Dubarry, Prof?'

Prof had merely stared, frowned, grunted and gone back to touring the layout of the Split Spurs, its saloon bar, storage spaces, entrances and exits and accommodation, Jay Matlan sweating and buzzing in his wake like an irritated fly.

There had been no further talk or contact between them as Quantril and his sidekicks had spent the long, hot afternoon settling in. The hostages had been bundled quickly out of sight, Jake stumbling and near to collapsing every step of the short distance from boardwalk to a room above the bar, Jessie walking silently, dead-eyed and grey, her frequent spasms of shivering shaking her whole body.

Prof had ordered a close watch on the suddenly plentiful supply of free liquor available. 'Keep your heads clear,' he had ordered, his wet, beady gaze honing its edge on Rimms McCane and Jason Stock, 'or leastways as clear as they've ever been. And just because we've got some pretty bar girls to hand, that ain't an excuse to over-indulge. We're not here for pleasure.'

But Abigail doubted if the pronouncement meant more than words to be heard, not listened to. McCane and Stock already had roving eyes and itchy fingers, with Charlie Loome only half a step behind them.

Abigail had at first wandered the saloon with the authority of the senior bar girl she had become, comforting the younger girls and trying, best she could, to reassure that all would be well given time. She had been under the almost constant gaze of Quantril with no chance, as she was planning, of establishing exactly where Jake and Jessie were being held. If she could find out for certain, perhaps make some contact. . . .

But it was at that moment, with Abigail already at the foot of the stairs to the rooms, when Stock had discovered Eli and Harry Macks among the barrels, crates and stores outback.

Matlan had pleaded the men's innocence. 'They ain't nothin' but a couple of old town gophers scroungin' around back of the bar for whatever comes up. You know the sort of fellas. Hell, most towns have 'em, but they don't mean no harm.'

The appeal had fallen on deaf ears, particularly where Prof was concerned. 'We'll deal with them in a way that Bandyrock ain't likely to forget,' had been the finality of his pronouncement.

The thinner night air cooled Abigail's brow but not her thoughts or the images they held of the shooting of Harry Macks. She stifled a shiver and turned from the sight of the dark street, the flickering glow of a lantern in Wheeler's mercantile and the shadows that seemed alive with the staring eyes of Luke Quantril.

It was time, she decided, to act.

'They were good days back there in Dubarry,' grinned Quantril as Abigail drew level with the corner table he had commandeered. He blew a cloud of smoke, examined the glowing tip of his cigar, then raised his eyes in the same devouring stare. 'You agree?' he asked.

Abigail twitched but hid the shiver behind it. 'I get a mite selective these days about what I do and don't recall,' she answered loftily.

Quantril's grin widened to a smile that darkened almost instantly to a sneer. 'Don't get smart, lady. I ain't in the mood.'

'I'm sure you're not, Mr Quantril,' said Abigail, summoning her most winsome saloon-bar smile. 'You've got matters on your mind. Weighty matters, I'd reckon. Much like you had in Dubarry, if memory serves me well. And you know somethin', mister, you ain't handlin' these any better than you did all them years back. Don't learn a deal, do you?'

Abigail felt the softest, iciest trickle of sweat easing

down her spine. She had maybe pushed her luck too far, she thought, watching fearfully as Quantril came slowly, menacingly to his feet, the palm of one hand flat on the table.

Jason Stock lounging nearby began to titter. Rimms McCane pushed his hat to the back of his head and hooked his thumbs in his belt. 'Sassy lady, ain't she, Luke?' he quipped.

The bar girls gathered at the far end of the room, grouped in a tighter, darker clutch. Jay Matlan mopped his brow on a stained glasscloth.

Quantril blew a line of smoke. 'I could get to refreshin' your memories of Dubarry a whole lot sharper,' he growled, coming to his full height, the sweat gleaming on his face.

'Leave it,' ordered Prof emerging from the shadowy depths of the bar as if splintered from the darkness. 'This ain't the time,' he added, adjusting the set of his derby. 'We'll get to the reckonin' soon enough.' He glared at Stock. 'Go take over from Charlie watchin' over our assets. And stay awake.' The glare softened. 'We've got a long night to get through. Let's not waste our energy, eh?'

'Drinks on the house!' offered Matlan with a flourish of the glasscloth.

'I'll say when we drink,' croaked Prof, his cheeks beginning to glow.

Abigail shrugged, tossed her hair to her neck and flounced to the bar with an exaggerated wiggle of her hips. 'You fellas please yourselves,' she smiled, moving behind the bar to the array of bottles and glasses on the back shelf, 'but I'm for a drink – assuming I am not offending you, Professor.'

Prof merely glowered as Abigail poured a large measure of whiskey and raised the glass to the watching faces. 'A toast,' she announced. 'To the future – in whatever shape it comes.' She downed the drink in one noisy gulp, thudded the glass to the bar and sighed deeply, her eyes already scanning the shelves beneath the counter.

Where was it, she wondered, her gaze flicking left to right? It was always here – the safety gun; the loaded derringer Matlan insisted on being to hand against the threat of an awkward customer. She stepped forward as if to reach for a cloth, touched a small pile of them in a darkened part of the shelf and felt the solid mass of the gun.

It was under her skirts and safe in her garter long before Prof had removed the bottle and started to pour the contents across the floor.

'Such a waste,' smiled Abigail, easing back to the bar and then, without another word or glance, moving with provocatively measured steps to the foot of the stairs.

TWELVE

A thin, hazy mist had drifted out of the Bluespecks at the first hint of light. It shifted and hung like breath low to the street, sidled in slow bands and ribbons across the boardwalks, rooftops, doors and fencing and flattened into grey featureless faces at the windows.

From the window in his office Sheriff Connell had watched the street, the shadows and the faint glow of light at the Split Spurs for most of the night. There had been few movements save for Stock's occasional breaks on the boardwalk from the smoke-filled saloon bar, McCane's lounging stance at the batwings and the bar girls flitting through the shadowy light like moths.

What had become of Abigail, Connell had wondered? Had she some plan to get close to Jake and Jessie, and what now was their condition? How long before Quantril made another move? Had the gang a time and day for leaving Bandyrock? Could they afford to linger? But how many more bodies would lie in the same bloody and fly-infested dirt as Harry Macks before Quantril eventually pulled out?

'And what we goin' to do about collectin' the money for them scumbags?' Doc had asked, stirring himself from his doze at the sheriff's desk. 'Quantril's patience on that count is goin' to be on a pretty short fuse, if you ask me. I'd figure for him and Prof wantin' to leave town as fast as they can.' He had joined Connell at the window. 'I wonder if there really is a posse ridin' out of Morristown or Gentry? Might be the answer to our prayers.'

'Yeah, well, don't hang your hat on it, Doc. We start pinnin' our hopes in that direction we ain't goin' to get nowhere. We've got to face things exactly as they are here and now – and save as many lives as possible. Them sidekicks of Quantril's are all for shootin' first and askin' questions later, if at all. So let's keep things as easy and steady as we can. I don't want nobody steppin' out of line, not for no reason. Pass the word again, and don't let nobody forget.'

Sheriff Connell stretched, stifled a yawn and hitched his pants. 'As for collectin' the money, I don't fancy it'll be long before Quantril gives his orders.'

Nor was it. The hill mist still lingered and the sun had not yet burned its warmth through to the deserted street and quiet buildings, when the batwings swung open on a bluster of bodies as Rimms McCane and Charlie Loome lugged a table and chair from the bar, across the boardwalk to the dirt. Following in the wake of the grunting sidekicks was Prof with Luke Quantril at his side, a primed and gleaming Winchester in his grip.

'Shift your butt, lawman!' shouted Quantril, at the

same time releasing a volley of shots high into the grey morning light. 'We got business to attend to and I ain't for messin'.' He lowered the rifle, snapped his orders to McCane and Loome and glared like a hungry hawk at the sheriff's office.

The blaze of shots had brought Connell and Doc Merry to the boardwalk before the echo of them had faded.

'What now?' groaned Doc, narrowing his still-sleepy gaze on the table and chair.

Bernard Wheeler struggled into his coat as he closed the door on his store and stared wide-eyed into the street. Adam Levens hurried from the livery to join the group of townsmen making a slow, cautious way to the Split Spurs.

Eli limped from the shadows of an alley to join Wheeler. 'What in tarnation are they plannin' now?'

'We're goin' to find out soon enough,' murmured the storekeeper. 'Don't move 'til we get a signal from the sheriff.'

'You've got no worries on that count,' grunted Eli.

Quantril raised the rifle again but only to draw the onlookers' full attention. 'All right,' he called, his gaze taking in the watching faces, 'here's how it is. Sheriff Connell's goin' to sit at this table here and be the collector; and you – every last one of you livin' and breathin' in this two-bit town – are goin' to file past him leaving all your money right there on the table, Sheriff can read and write, so he'll be keepin' a record for Prof to peruse.'

'Hell's teeth!' muttered Doc. 'He'll never get away with it.'

'See if he don't,' said Connell, taking a step forward into the street. 'We do exactly as he says. There's no choice.'

Quantril continued to glare round the street and the steadily filling boardwalks as the townsfolk stirred into life and moved tentatively from their homes to the light.

Quantril swaggered to the middle of the street. 'And don't nobody get to thinkin' they can cheat or wriggle out on this. My boys and Prof here will be watchin' every move and countin' every dollar.' He spun round to face Wheeler at the mercantile. 'You, storekeeper, you're goin' to make a whole heap bigger donation. We'll be wantin' supplies to see us clear through to the border and beyond. Prof's made a list. See that he gets all he wants and no arguin'.'

Wheeler glanced despairingly at Sheriff Connell. 'I ain't so sure—' he croaked.

'Well, you'd just better be, and fast,' growled Quantril. 'Otherwise, mister, that store of yours won't be standin' come nightfall. Do I make myself clear?'

Wheeler simply swallowed and nodded.

'And we're goin' to need fresh horses when the time comes.' Quantril swung round again, levelling the barrel of the rifle at Levens. 'You make sure we have, right? Fresh horses and trail packs, and your money.' He grinned and prodded the barrel into space. 'You should think yourself lucky to be alive.'

Doc Merry took three fast strides into the street.

'To hell with you wantin' this, demandin' that,' he blustered. 'What about the old man and his daughter? I insist on lookin' to 'em. Now!'

71

'All in good time, Doc, all in good time.' Prof grinned, tipping the angle of his derby. 'You have my word they're alive. That's good enough for now. Meantime, we have other priorities. I suggest we don't waste any more time.'

Abigail watched and waited at the saloon-bar window that overlooked the street. She had heard Quantril's shouted orders, cringed at Prof's preening himself for his counting-house role to come, tried to catch a glimpse of Sheriff Connell's expression as he crossed to the table and chair arranged in the street, Doc Merry's seething anger, Wheeler's indignation – and then hissed her own curse to herself and turned to face the half-dozen bar girls huddled behind her.

'Now listen up here,' she whispered, glancing quickly round the bar to the stairs and the balcony above them where Jason Stock hovered on guard outside the room holding Jake and Jessie. Abigail's gaze concentrated on the girls again. 'We're in this up to our necks,' she continued, 'and there ain't no turning from it. But – a big "but" – there might be a chance for them poor folk up there if we work together. You with me?'

The girls nodded, their eyes beginning to gleam.

'Right. So here's my thinking. . . .' She ushered the girls towards a deeper, darker corner under the watchful stare of Matlan who, sensing the need for privacy, busied himself with a glasscloth.

'Them scumbags are holding Jessie and her pa in that spare room at the back. You know the one: far end, part-furnished, windows boarded up. A hell-hole.

Now, question is: how we going to get that rat Stock away from the door for long enough for me to get into the room and out again without him knowing?'

A red-headed girl tossed the tousled locks of her hair across her shoulders. 'Same way as you get men to do most things,' she quipped with a wink.

'I figured you'd opt for that,' grinned Abigail. 'Stock-in-trade, eh?'

'Doing what comes naturally, ain't it?' piped a girl at the back.

'But what are you planning, Abi?' urged another anxiously. 'Ain't you going to need a piece?'

'Got one,' said Abigail, patting the bulge of the weapon secure in her garter. 'Plan is to get to Jake and Jessie and get them out – if we can.'

'Hell,' gulped the girl, 'that ain't going to be no picnic. We all saw what happened to Harry Macks and Eli.'

Abigail bit at her lip. 'I know, but it's still a chance we've got to take. We owe it to Jessie.' She nodded to Matlan at the bar, listened to the orders still being shouted in the street, then led the girls to the foot of the stairs.

'Time to go to work, I think,' she smiled.

THIRTEEN

'That's all I have, every last cent.' The man threw the leather pouch to the table, watched as Sheriff Connell laid a hand reluctantly across it, then glowered at Quantril until his eyes were bloodshot with anger. 'My woman there's got what she stands in. There's nothin' else, 'ceptin' the shack back of Mr Wheeler's store. You can check for yourself.'

'There won't be no need for that, Matt,' said Connell. 'I know your situation.'

'I'll make the decisions, lawman,' spat Quantril. 'How much in the bag?'

'Forty dollars,' seethed the town man. 'Ain't you goin' to count it? Or mebbe you can't count, eh? Mebbe all you can do—'

'Move along, Matt,' urged Connell. 'You ain't makin' things any easier.'

The man scowled, stepped clear of the table and was helped on his way by a punch across the neck from Rimms McCane.

'Next,' snapped Quantril. 'And get a move on.'

An old-timer in baggy pants, a torn shirt and wearing a floppy-brimmed hat, shuffled to the table 'Five dollars exact,' he sprayed through broken teeth, throwing the money across the sheriff's list. He thrust his hands into the pockets of his pants and pulled them inside out. 'Not a bean more, so I don't know how I'm supposed to eat. You got any bright ideas, mister?'

Quantril spat. 'Try the scrub in them god-forsaken hills back of you.'

Prof smiled and tilted his hat. McCane twirled a Colt in his fingers. Charlie Loome rubbed his gut and winced.

'You know somethin',' said the old-timer, smacking his lips. 'I might just do that. Take myself on a long walk through the Bluespecks. You never know, I might just get to meetin' up with that posse that's sure to be high-tailin' it this way!'

'Out of my sight, old man,' grunted Quantril.

The man winked at Sheriff Connell and shuffled to the shadowed boardwalk where Doc Merry and Bernard Wheeler had been watching proceedings in a sullen silence.

'Two spits to a tin mug I'd take that old buffalo blaster of mine and blow them scum into kingdom come,' said the man, wafting a hand at the brim of his floppy hat. 'We just goin' to stand here and let this happen?'

The storekeeper rolled his shoulders beneath his frock-coat. 'You heard the sheriff. We have no choice.'

'For now,' added Doc Merry sharply. 'Sooner or later somethin's goin' to change – or somebody's goin' to make it change.'

The old-timer backed to the comforts of a chair in the deeper shade, swept the seat clear of flies and sat down. 'Don't seem possible to be witnessin' this,' he sighed. 'Hell, I've seen some things in my time – Plains wars, sharp-shootin' bounty hunters, big-eyed kids with a hankerin' for gunslingin', hangin's, beatin's, fire and famine – but this takes some bite of the biscuit and that's for certain.' He smacked his lips again. 'I just hope Jake and that pretty young gal of his are hangin' on back there.'

Doc's gaze narrowed on the batwings at the Split Spurs saloon. 'Mebbe it's time we got to takin' a look for ourselves,' he murmured. 'And I mean a *real* look.'

'Easy there, Doc,' cautioned Wheeler. 'We don't want no heroics. And the last thing we want is for our doc to be flattened there in the dirt.'

'I know, I know. I ain't for takin' no risks, but I've got to do somethin'.'

Doc Merry adjusted his hat, smoothed his coat and stepped into the sunlight.

Abigail flounced along the balcony above the bar, called for some hush among her giggling girls grouped at the head of the stairs, and glanced quickly out of the corner of her eye at Jason Stock standing guard at the door to her left.

The man was confused. His concentration had lapsed and now, with the first gleam of a beading of sweat on his brow, he was torn between grabbing one of the girls and leaving his post, or blazing a hail of shots to the ceiling in his anger and frustration.

'Now, now, girls, let's hurry this along some shall

we?' smiled Abigail, moving towards the group. 'Doesn't take all day to change our dresses and tidy up, does it?'

The girls cascaded into another bout of giggling and high-pitched chatter. Stock licked his lips, swallowed and shifted his weight to one hip. Abigail opened the door to her room and gestured for the girls to enter. 'Get what you need and use my room.' She smiled again. 'We don't want to upset the gentleman posted guard there, do we?' She glanced at Stock. 'Don't suppose there's any chance of looking to Jessie, is there? Just quickly. I wouldn't dally none.'

'No chance,' clipped Stock. 'Just do what you've got to do and make it fast.'

'Sure, sure,' soothed Abigail, urging the girls to the room.

She carefully and deliberately left the door open, encouraged the girls to keep up their chatter and giggling, checked the safety of the derringer in her garter and stood back against the wall to wait.

How long before Stock's curiosity got the better of him? How long before the sounds of the giggling and chatter proved too much and the images he was already conjuring led him away from the door to the back room?

Abigail stifled a shiver, urged the girls not to hurry, then tensed at the sudden scuff of a boot on board, the sound of slow, approaching steps.

Doc Merry stared down the barrel of Luke Quantril's levelled Colt, and shrugged. 'Pull that trigger if you're minded,' he said, his gaze steady on Quantril's face, 'but it ain't goin' to make a smack of difference. You're still goin' to have the same problem, so you don't score none, do you?'

The snaking file of townsfolk moving towards the table in the middle of the hot, dusty street had come to a halt. Sheriff Connell sat in silence, his eyes working quickly from Quantril to the Prof, then to the doc, the file of people, the shadows and shapes behind the sun's glare.

'So what'll it be?' asked Doc. 'Do I get to takin' a look at the girl and her pa in the name of human decency, or do you continue to leave them to rot? Choice is yours, Quantril, but I tell you now, straight, that young woman back there ain't goin' to be one spit of use to you dead.'

Quantril steadied the aim of the Colt and glared like a rattler for what seemed an endless minute. 'You all through?' he croaked at last. 'Can't you see I'm busy? Can't you get it into your numbskull head—'

'He's mebbe got a point,' said Prof, fingering the knot of his bandanna. 'We need the girl alive, and for some time yet. Let Charlie take the doc to her.'

Quantril waited a moment, then spun the Colt through his fingers and holstered it with a thud. 'One step out of line, mister, and Charlie will be takin' a look at the colour of your blood.'

Loome's gun cleared its leather to his grip as he gestured for Doc to walk towards the saloon.

'And make it quick,' snapped Quantril. 'It's time we put our backs to this two-bits town.'

Doc and the sidekick had taken no more than a half-dozen steps to the saloon when the scream from an upstairs room fronting the street pierced the morning heat like the cry of a strangled hawk.

Charlie Loome halted, the drawn Colt's barrel probing instantly in readiness for a target.

'What the hell,' murmured Doc under his tightening breath, conscious now of Loome at his shoulder.

'Don't move,' mouthed the sidekick, at the same time turning his head to glance at Quantril for his orders.

Rimms McCane had already positioned himself to face the suddenly restive file of townsfolk. Prof merely tweeked the folds of his bandanna.

'If Stock's gettin' into another bout of womanizin' fever . . .' he growled.

'Settle it, Charlie. Get that doc in there and quieten them gals.' He swung back to the sheriff at the table and the line of bewildered people 'And just what are we waitin' for here? Shift!'

Another scream from the room echoed across the street as Doc hurried forward under the prodding urgency of Loome's Colt. Glass shattered. A door thudded. More screaming, this time from more than one girl.

Doc stumbled in his anxiety, cursed, blinked furiously through a lathering of sweat and stumbled again to the anger of Loome at his heels.

'F'cris'sake, keep your feet, can't you?' spat the gunslinger, but was himself losing his balance in the next moment as the batwings at the bar crashed open and Jay Matlan sprawled across the boardwalk.

'Somebody get in there fast before—' he groaned only to be silenced by the crack of two shots, a scream, a howling roar, the thuds and scrapes of chairs and tables being thrown aside, and then a sudden quiet before the batwings opened again.

Jake Wardman hit the street dirt in a twist of loose limbs and ragged clothes and did not move.

FOURTEEN

'Bleedin's stopped, but that leg's in one helluva mess.' Doc Merry pushed at his rolled shirtsleeves and peered closer into Jake Wardman's ashen face. 'Ain't goin' to ask how you're feelin', I can see, but if it's any consolation you got lucky there. Wonder to me is that scumbag Stock didn't plug you straight through the gut.'

Jake opened his eyes and winced as he stirred in the chair at the back of the saloon bar where Doc and Jay Matlan had been ordered to carry him.

'I'll get to him and that daughter of his when I'm through here,' Quantril had growled from the street. 'Watch over 'em, Charlie, and keep Jason away from the women.'

'Easy, easy,' soothed Doc in little more than a whisper to Jake's ear, conscious of Loome hovering close by. 'And before you ask, Jessie's all right,' he went on. 'Don't you fret none now, you hear? We're goin' to come through this. So just stay calm, real calm.'

Doc turned, nodded briefly to reassure Matlan of Jake's survival, then concentrated his gaze on Abigail and her girls gathered at the far end of the bar. He crossed quickly to the shivering group, disregarding Charlie Loome's watchful gaze.

'What happened here, Abi?' he hissed. 'You heard what the sheriff said. Could've gotten yourself killed.'

Abigail fingered a developing bruise on her cheek. 'Just felt we had to do something,' she croaked, her voice grating like a worn wheel. 'I found the derringer behind the bar; thought we could divert Stock while I got to Jake and Jessie. We did, but not for long enough. He sprung to what we were doin' and . . .' She fingered the bruise again. 'It ended like you see. But, hell, wouldn't have wished that on Jake.'

'His leg's a mess, but he'll survive,' said Doc. 'What about Jessie? How's she?'

'Darn near out of her mind. Maybe right out of it already. I don't know how much more she can take. Do you reckon—'

'Let's cut the talk, shall we?' growled Loome, swaggering across the bar.

'I need to see the girl,' insisted Doc.

Loome settled a hand on the butt of his holstered Colt and relaxed his weight. 'Forget it,' he grinned. 'I got strict orders and we're stickin' to 'em. Stock is lookin' to the girl again. Teachin' her a lesson in good manners, l shouldn't wonder.' He aimed a fount of spittle to a spittoon. 'Meantime, you can get back there to the street. I'll call you if you're needed.'

Doc's fists clenched. 'I just hope that when your time comes, as it surely will, that nobody, not nobody, shows you one blink of mercy.' His cheeks deepened to a fiery crimson. 'You ain't worth it, mister,' he added. 'In fact you ain't worth nothin' to nobody!'

Doc swung round and banged through the batwings to the boardwalk like a sudden draught of angry wind.

The day wore grimly on for the townsfolk of Bandyrock, passing from a heat-filled morning to the blaze of midday and the languid hours of a suffocating afternoon.

Quantril kept up his demand for money, marshalling the line of men and women under the beady-eyed scrutiny of Prof until, one by one, they had been fleeced of every dollar they could muster, questioned, prodded and searched and finally dismissed only when every last cent had been recorded, counted and deposited in the money-bag to the gloating satisfaction of Prof.

Sheriff Connell had said little, save to console the distressed as best he was allowed by Quantril, and quieten the angry, but his gaze between recording and counting had missed nothing of what he could see of the comings and goings at the saloon, the faces of the townsfolk, the street and the deepening shadows.

He had managed only a few words with Doc Merry.

'Done the best I can in there,' Doc had murmured at his shoulder, 'but Jake's in a poor way. He ain't goin' to be fit to travel on. As for Jessie – no sayin'. Abigail only did what she thought would help. I tell you straight—'

But a shove across the back from Rimms McCane had moved Doc on to the boardwalk where Eli, Adam Levens and Bernard Wheeler were gathered in the deepest shadows outside the mercantile.

'We're workin' on a plan,' hissed Eli, shielding his mouth in the flat of his hand. 'You wanna hear?'

'Not if it involves misplaced heroics and more shootin'.' Doc frowned, his stare, as cold as ice, on the table in the street, the slumped shuffling townsfolk, Quantril, Prof, and the gun-toting Rimms McCane. 'But if there was some way of poisonin' them rats for the vermin they are—'

'That's just what we were thinkin'!' beamed Eli, smacking his lips 'How'd you guess?'

'Forget it,' said Doc. 'You ain't never goin' to get the chance. Soon as Quantril's bled us as far as he reckons he can go, he'll ride for the border. And that ain't goin' to be long in comin'.' His frown deepened. 'Question is, will he take Jake in the state he's in, or leave him and hold on to Jessie 'til he's clear?'

'And then what?' asked the blacksmith. 'You ain't figurin' on him turnin' the gal loose just like that, are you?'

'We're goin' to have to raise enough riders to trail 'em every yard of the way,' said Wheeler, fidgeting with the lapels of his coat. 'If somebody ain't there, chances are we'll never see Jessie again.'

'Or our money,' quipped Eli.

Doc grunted. 'If only we could be certain somebody had ridden out of Morristown or Gentry. If we knew for a fact that a posse had reached the Bluespecks. . . .'

'Well, mebbe we could make certain,' murmured Levens. 'Mebbe we've still got the time while Quantril and that Professor fella can't see no further than the next dollar.'

'What you sayin'?' said Wheeler.

'I've still got horses stabled back there at the livery. I've still got tack. Them rats haven't got to fleecin' me of them yet, so who's to say we can't put 'em to our use? The blacksmith's voice slid to a softer tone. 'If we could get a rider clear of town and into the Bluespecks unknown to Quantril and his sidekicks, he might succeed in makin' contact with any searchin' posse.'

'And if he did,' added Wheeler, 'he'd be able to lead them on a direct course to the trail Quantril takes when he pulls out of here.'

'Exactly,' said Levens. 'Could save the posse a helluva lot of time and wasted trailin' *and* add some needed guns to whatever we do when Connell gets to plannin' it. What do you reckon, Doc?'

'It's about the only sensible thing we can actually do that's been suggested so far,' said Doc, still watching the street. He waited a moment before turning to the others. 'Who's goin' to do the ridin'?'

'Me,' offered. Eli, hardly stopping to take breath. 'And no arguin'. After what me and Harry tried to do and seein' Harry sprawled out there in the dirt like some two-bit dead turkey, I owe it to him and the town, Jake and Jessie and Abigail, all of you. So let's get me a horse and out of town while there's still a couple of hours of good light. Agreed? You reckon we can do it? Ain't nobody goin' to miss me if I ride out now.'

'We'll do it – the hell we will!' grinned Adam. 'Follow me.'

FIFTEEN

The line of silent townsfolk shuffling their slow way to the table in the hot dusty street had dwindled to barely a dozen when Prof called a sudden halt.

'That'll do,' he announced, scooping the last of the money to the bag. 'Time's gettin' short and we got other arrangements to look to.'

Quantril ordered the folk to move on. 'You got lucky,' he sneered, pulling an old man aside to grab the small pouch clutched in his hand. 'But I'll take this all the same. Buy myself a few bottles for when I'm luxuriatin' on that southern hacienda I'm plannin'.'

Rimms McCane scanned the street, his Colt still tight in his grip. 'You want I should go shake that black-smith into life and get ourselves some fresh mounts?'

'Later,' grunted Prof. 'We'll attend to provisions first.'

'I hope you ain't figurin' on trailin' Jake Wardman to the border,' said Connell, coming to his feet at the table. 'Doc reckons he ain't in no state to be moved. You'd have a dead body on your hands within hours.'

Prof heaved the money-bag from the table. 'You can

have him, Sheriff,' he smiled thinly. 'We take the girl – and Abigail.'

'Abigail?' protested Connell, the sweat wet and sticky on his face. 'But why, f'cris'sake? Ain't one enough for you? What's the point—'

'You heard the man,' snapped Quantril. 'We take the girl and Abigail. I've got some scores to settle with her.'

'And you'll release them at the border?' frowned Connell.

'Sure we will,' said Quantril with a dismissive wave of his hand. 'We'll release 'em. Don't doubt me, do you?'

They cleared the street as the shadows lengthened. The table and chair were carted back to the bar, the townsfolk shuffled home, some to hide, some to count their losses, others to give thanks that they were still alive. The silence crept in and Bandyrock waited.

'They're plannin' on pullin' out by nightfall,' said Wheeler, pacing quietly along the boardwalk fronting the sheriff's office. 'They'll take Jessie, Abigail, our money, stores and horses – and there ain't a darn thing we can do about it.' He turned to face the blacksmith. 'Eli get away clean enough?'

'No problem,' said Levens. 'Went as soft as a shadow. He'll be well clear and into the hills by now. Let's hope it's worth it.'

The storekeeper grunted and turned again to face the street and the first glimmer of lantern-light at the Split Spurs.

'Doc's down there now tendin' to Jake. But hell,

what about Jessie, what state's she in, and how's Abigail goin' to face things? She ain't the sort for givin' in or takin' orders from the likes of Quantril and his scum. She'll fight. She won't go under.'

'Better not fight too hard,' said Levens on a flatter note. 'Them rats ain't goin' to be for exercisin' patience once they hit that border. They'll kill as easy as spittin', specially when they figure for Jessie and Abi bein' witness to what happened here. You want my opinion—'

'Save it,' said Sheriff Connell, stepping from his office. 'We got other things to be doin'.' He strode to the edge of the boardwalk. 'Adam, you get back to your livery and make certain Quantril and his men don't get the pick of the fresh horses. We're goin' to need the best we can lay our hands on if we're goin' to mount our own posse.'

'You got it, Frank,' said Adam adjusting his hat as he moved away. 'Consider it done.'

Connell nodded and gestured for Wheeler to follow him into his office where a low-trimmed lantern lit the room with a soft glow.

The sheriff spread his hands across a large, worn and cracked animal skin on which, in a faded, spidery scrawl, words and lines had been scratched as if by the sharpened end of a twig dipped in blood.

'What in tarnation is that?' Wheeler peered close, frowning.

'Knew I still had it some place,' said Connell, his gaze deepening to intrigue as he stared at the skin. 'Had it given to me by an old-time silver-miner when I first hit the Bluespecks out of Kimberly. Said he thought I might find it useful some day, same as he had after he'd been given it by the leader of a Navajo huntin' party.'

'Fascinatin',' grunted the storekeeper, 'but what precisely is it?' He straightened, tugging impatiently at his coat. 'We ain't exactly blessed with time for examin-in' the history of some Navajo scratchin's, so mebbe—'

'Well, you hold it right there, Mr Wheeler,' cautioned Connell with the lift of a hand. 'These ain't just any old scratchin's. Not nohow they ain't. These could be the difference between life and death for young Jessie and Miss Abigail out there.'

Doc Merry closed and locked his medicine-bag, tapped his fingers on the worn leather for a moment, then took a firm grip on the handle and set his icy gaze on Luke Quantril. One last try, he thought, forced to blink on the steadily thickening smoke and booze haze of the Split Spurs' saloon bar. He was never going to get another. This would be it. What the hell!

He took another careful look at Jake Wardman sleeping fitfully in the corner of the bar, at Abigail and her girls hardly daring to move under the consuming gaze of Rimms McCane, cleared his throat deliberately and crossed to the table where Luke Quantril, Prof and Charlie Loome were demolishing the last of a bottle of Jay Matlan's best whiskey.

'I ain't for sayin' this again—' he began.

'Then don't,' clipped Loome, fingering the wet rim around the top of his glass.

89

Doc stiffened. 'Like I say, this is for the last time of askin'. I need to see the girl you're holdin' up there. If she's for travellin' on all them miles to the border, through God knows what sort of heat you're goin' to suffer once you hit the desert, then I have a right to look to her, bearin' in mind the condition I imagine she's in.' He swallowed and licked quickly at a dribble of sweat. 'I'm askin' in the name of human decency,' he added softly.

Loome chuckled. Quantril gulped at his drink.

Prof leaned back in his chair and stared benevolently into Doc's glazed eyes. 'Naturally,' he smiled, tapping the brim of his derby. 'Of course. You're a man of medicine; you care for folk. So, yes, by all means see her. Right now.'

He leaned forward. 'Not that it'll do either of you any good. We're pullin' out. But no harm done in sayin' goodbye, is there?'

SIXTEEN

'Tracks, as old as time itself, and every one of them tried and tested.' Sheriff Connell's finger moved slowly, precisely over the lines scratched on the skin. 'Huntin' tracks, Mr Wheeler, as used for centuries by the Navajo.'

The storekeeper grunted, screwed his eyes in concentration through the shadowy lantern-light in the sheriff's office and followed the moving finger.

'See,' Connell continued, 'from here, just short of what we know as Pale Rock Creek, to there, Pryor's Gulch, and on through the pines.'

'Yes, yes, I see all that,' said Wheeler impatiently, 'and like I say, it's fascinatin', but right now we have the whole town and its folk under threat and likely—'

'But this is the one,' persisted the sheriff, disregarding Wheeler's sigh. 'Here, from what, when it was first scratched, would have been the site of Bandyrock as we know it today, through Sleeping Valley and then, would you believe it, bearin' way out to the east at the Sky Point Range clear through to the border. An unknown trail. Day and a half's ride at most.'

Wheeler swallowed and concentrated. 'I couldn't reach the border from here usin' the old desert trail in under three days, not even with a fast horse,' he murmured, his eyes gleaming in the glow.

'Exactly,' said Connell, standing to his full height at the table.

Wheeler waited a moment, still staring at the skin. 'Let me get this straight,' he began. 'I reckon for you figurin' that if we rode out to this old Navajo huntin' trail – assumin' we could find it or that it's still there – we could trail ahead of Quantril and be at the border at least a whole day before him? That it? Is that the point of all this?'

'Almost, 'ceptin' this is a job for one man. A whole posse of riders scourin' around for the track would be a hindrance and they'd damage more than they'd find. No, one man movin' ahead as a welcomin' party for when Quantril hits his promised land, while the rest follow along the desert trail, is a chance we can't afford to turn our backs on. We've got to take it.'

'And that one man bein' – yourself?'

'I wouldn't ask or expect anyone else to do it. This is my show, my privilege as the law around here. And, in any case, this is mine.' He tapped a finger on the skin. 'No argument, eh?'

'No argument. No point,' agreed Wheeler. 'But in the meantime—'

'Hold it,' said Connell, crossing quickly from the table to the window 'Things are movin' at the saloon. If Quantril's ready for pullin' out, let's not delay him.'

Luke Quantril, Prof, Charlie Loome and Rimms
McCane lined the boardwalk fronting the Split Spurs
saloon like buzzards awaiting a banquet.

The soft lantern-light filtering from the bar behind
them cast their stiff, unmoving shadows into the street
where they lay like beams of black iron. Their gazes
were tight and almost unblinking, their expressions
flat and without the slightest flicker of emotion.

Quantril was the first to speak to the handful of
townsfolk, Sheriff Connell and Bernard Wheeler gathered in the deepening night gloom.

'We're ridin' just as soon as that blacksmith stirs his
butt out of the livery there. We'll be gone inside the
hour. The girl and the bar whore – now bein' looked
to by Mister Stock – will ride with us, but you've got my
word on it they'll be freed at the border.'

'Lyin' sonofabitch,' muttered Wheeler under his
breath. 'Them girls have got about as much chance—'

'Easy there,' murmured Connell. 'Let 'em go.
We're goin' to be busy the minute they clear town.'

Quantril had taken a step forward from the others,
his eyes gleaming through the shadow darkening his
face. 'You folk should consider yourselves fortunate,'
he went on. 'In view of your co-operation, Prof here
has persuaded me not to torch your town.'

'And he would've too,' seethed Wheeler again.

'How about that?' grinned Quantril, his gaze
settling for a moment on Sheriff Connell. 'Lucky, ain't
you? But don't you go spoilin' it none by ridin' in our
tracks to the border, or figurin' on raisin' guns from
some other quarter. Minute I, or Prof, or the boys here
reckon on us bein' followed the girl dies. You got that?

You hearin' me clear? The girl dies.' His gaze burned in its scan of the faces in the street, settled again on Connell and then on Bernard Wheeler. 'You get that store of yours open, mister, and you let Prof and my men help themselves. Now!'

'Do it,' hissed the sheriff, urging Wheeler to move.

Quantril stood his ground as Prof and McCane stepped towards the store.

Charlie Loome sauntered slowly in their wake, pausing when he reached Connell. 'I've been trailin' back of my memory for a recollection of you, mister,' he mouthed drily. 'And you know somethin', I'm gettin' the distinct impression I should kill you right now while I've still got the chance.'

Connell stiffened, his gaze cold, a trickle of hot sweat stinging in his neck. 'You shouldn't spoil a good mind,' he said as if spitting out the words. 'Be assured I shan't when the time comes.'

Loome was on the verge of a retort when Quantril's orders snapped across the gloom. 'Get to it, Charlie, we ain't got all night.'

The sidekick moved on. Connell relaxed but only momentarily as Doc Merry, his shirtsleeves rolled to the elbows, the sweat gleaming on his furrowed brow, pushed through the batwings and without a word to Quantril stepped into the street and took the longest, deepest breath of his life.

'Jake's goin' to need some close nursin'. His fears for Jessie ain't helpin' one mite. As for the girl . . .' Doc mopped an already damp bandanna over his face and sighed. 'Yeah, well, if she makes it to the border it'll be little short of a miracle. I've seen her and she ain't a pretty sight. Only consolation we've got – if you can call it that – is that Abigail's goin' to be with her, though God knows what treatment she's goin' to face.'

Doc pocketed the bandanna, eased the set of his hat and turned his tired gaze back to the saloon. 'They're goin' to be needin' me right up to pullin' out,' he murmured darkly. 'Best get to 'em. We'll shift Jake soon as we can. You got any plans for a posse?'

'We've got a plan. Best we've had,' said Connell. 'Bernard will fill you in soon as he's all through at the store.'

Doc nodded and walked quietly away to the saloon, pausing for a moment when he reached Quantril. 'Sooner you're out of this town the better,' he croaked. 'Place is beginnin' to smell!'

Quantril stared, muttered under his breath, but stayed silent at Prof's bidding with a grip on his gun hand.

'Have no fear, Doc,' smiled Quantril, 'we shall be gone long before the moon is climbin' on them hills back of you. We shall be headin' south, our needs here met, our acquaintance with your town concluded. And I certainly shan't be sorry. Nevertheless, you have served a purpose; a means to an end, as they say.'

The smile faded, the gaze hardened to a glare, a cheek muscle twitched. 'Now just get the hell into that two-bit saloon and get that young girl ready to ride,' he growled. 'And if she ain't lookin' good time we're set to pull out, I shall hold you personally responsible.' He took a step closer to focus the glare directly into Doc's eyes. 'Just remember, Doc, it ain't too late for

95

me to change my mind and leave this place no more than a windblown scatterin' of ashes. The boys would like that, so I suggest you go very, very carefully, like steppin' through cactus. Get me?'

The five men mounted up in silence, Jessie Wardman and Abigail hand-roped to trail mounts led by Rimms McCane and Jason Stock. Charlie Loome trailed the pack-horse at the rear of the party, with Quantril and Prof heading up the party like military generals.

Jessie, her weakened state worsening, had been carried to her horse and fixed in position like a sack of supplies. Doc Merry had insisted on being as close as the gunslingers would permit, but his heart had been heavy and his anger within a spit of boiling over into making what he knew would be a fatal move at the sight of the bedraggled and bewildered girl. Abigail had done her best to reassure that she would look to her whenever she was able, but like Doc, Sheriff Connell and the watching townsfolk of Bandyrock, she was all too aware that her own life was on the line. If she made it to the border she would have got lucky. But at what price?

'Let's ride!' shouted Quantril, and within minutes the shapes and sounds of the riders and horses hell-bent for the trail south were no more than ghosts on the moonlit night.

SEVENTEEN

The growl of a mountain lion echoed and faded through the hills and rocky peaks as if to lay claim to the night itself. Sheriff Connell patted the mare's neck, murmured soothingly into her pricked ears and reined her forward slowly to the faint narrow track. The horse responded with a gentle snort, the scuff of a hoof through dry scrub and a flick of the long, brushed tail.

Connell settled again to the careful search. He reckoned he was now some three hours out of town. He had trailed at a steady pace through the darkness along familiar tracks through the foothills, making fast progress to the first of the ridge line, then turning sharply into thin brush and scattered pines for the slopes to Sleeping Valley.

'That's where you'll hit your first problem,' Doc Merry had said, consulting the Navajo hunting map again after listening to Connell's tale of how he had come by it and what he was planning. 'Somewhere there,' he had continued, running a finger over the skin. 'I figure for an hour's ride out of town. Hit the ridge to the east, find the track and stay with it. Lookin' at this, I'd reckon for the trail to Sky Point bein' dead ahead of you from there on. But that's only surmisin', o' course.' He had paused a moment. 'You sure you want to do this alone?'

It had taken Connell less than a half-hour to saddle up, arm himself and leave his precise orders with Doc and Bernard Wheeler. 'Get together as strong a posse as you're able. No hangers-on, no riders who might not stay the pace. Secure the town and be on the desert trail by first light. Quantril's goin' to have a head start on you, but he's trailin' a pack-horse and the women so he's bound to be slowed up some. All you've got to do is stay with him at a safe distance and be real close when he hits the border.'

'And then?' Wheeler had asked.

'Frankly, I don't know,' Connell had answered. 'That's the truth.'

'And you?' Doc had murmured.

'Me? I'll see you at the border. Let's just hope Eli's made contact with a trailin' posse.'

'We ain't got much, have we?' Wheeler had grunted disconsolately.

'We've got damn all! But everythin' to fight for. . . .'

The mare moved quietly, steadily on, her feet finding the vague line of the track as if by instinct. Connell's eyes ached, in part from lack of sleep and partly due to the concentration of probing the darkness, watching for anything and everything that shifted in the shadows, or anything that might shift.

But his thoughts turned as if in a whirlwind: from the once quiet street and peaceful folk of Bandyrock, the day-to-day routine that, it had seemed, might never be disturbed, much less broken, to the discovery of the carnage at the Wardman homestead, the grisly reality of digging a grave for Martha, burying her, the grim realization of Jake and Jessie's fate as hostages to Quantril; the pillage of the town, the stealing of every man's last dollar, Charlie Loome's threat, the look on Abigail's face as the gang had ridden into the night, the despair in Jessie's eyes. . . .

The mare snorted and tossed her head.

Connell reined back, halted, watched and listened. Nothing moving that he could see, no sounds save those of the night-life seeking out its survival. His eyes narrowed again as he probed and squinted on the darkness wondering for the first time since leaving town if what he was doing, based on the faded lines of an ancient Navajo hunting map, was the wisest move to have made.

Maybe he should have stayed in town to help Doc, Wheeler, Adam Levens and the others organize the posse; or maybe he should have ridden out to join up with Eli. Maybe he should have done what was eating at his gut and twitching on the tip of every finger, and taken a chance, trusted his luck, and risked a shoot-out with Quantril and his sidekicks while they were still in his sights.

Or maybe not.

He grunted, patted the mare's neck and urged her forward. He was here now, he thought, rolling to the careful steps of the mount; this was the reality and he had to make it by sun-up to the foot of Sky Point.

An icy sweat prickled in his neck at the thought of

Jessie and Abigail riding ever deeper into the cold desert night.

Abigail winced at the bite of the pain in her spine, but buried it in a sigh of relief as Quantril raised an arm for the party to rein up.

'There's an outcrop to the left,' he announced across the thin night air. 'We'll rest the mounts a while before we push through to Snake Creek. That'll be the last waterin' hole 'til we reach the border.'

'On there!' cracked McCane, tugging on the rope to Abigail's mount.

Abigail stifled another wince and glanced quickly to what she could make out of the slumped shape of Jessie on the horse led by Stock. 'And go easy there, will you?' she snapped. 'The girl's all through, or don't that matter none now that you've got what you wanted?' She huffed and tossed her loose hair indignantly. 'Some big-time gunslingers, eh, standin' behind the skirts of an ordinary homestead girl! Make you feel good, does it? I ain't never seen nothin' so pathetic in grown men!'

'You want I should silence this lippy woman, Luke?' called McCane. 'I don't have a fancy for this all the way to the border.' He tugged the rope again and glared.

'Just stay with her,' said Quantril without looking back. 'I hear her plain enough, but she can mouth all she likes, she ain't goin' no place save south.'

'You hangin' on to her?' queried Stock. 'Don't tell me you're plannin' on takin' her across the border. Hell, there's goin' to be a whole heap of *señoritas* for the askin' once we hit the south. What you want to go trailin' some two-bit saloon whore for?'

'That's my business, mister,' quipped Quantril, his gaze fixed on the looming shapes of the outcrop ahead. 'Just do like I say.'

Stock flicked the reins impatiently. 'Well, I tell you straight, you ain't seein' me for Southern dust once I get my share of what Prof's huggin' to him there.'

'Same goes for me,' echoed McCane. 'I ain't for lingerin' in some mud-walled squat. I'm for the high sun and haciendas.' He laughed to himself. 'And just so's I can get to the dreamin', Prof, how much is my share goin' to come to? Kinda comfortin' to be knowin'.'

'I ain't got to the countin',' said Prof, his tight, narrowed stare unblinking in the moonlight.

There was a moment of silence. The soft scuff of hoofs, crack of leather and jangle of tack filled the night like sounds dropped through it.

'Don't leave it too long, Prof,' clipped Stock lightly but with an edge that could not be missed.

Abigail winced again as the party and the trailed pack-horse moved on to the outcrop, her mind spinning with thoughts of reaching the border and being forced to cross it. Alive.

EIGHTEEN

Doc Merry hurried through the still moonlit night from his clapboard home, where he had settled Jake Wardman in the care of his housekeeper, and crossed the street to the Split Spurs and the waiting posse.

Bernard Wheeler stepped urgently through the batwings to greet him. 'All set – leastways as much as we'll ever be,' he said, tapping the holster at his hip. 'Matt Holby has volunteered to stay behind and keep watch over the town.'

'So how many are ridin'?' asked Doc.

'Myself, you, Adam Levens, Jay Matlan, George King, Skip Marks, Art Toyne . . . Seven at the last count, and that's about as good as it'll get. We've got plenty who are willin' enough, but most are either too old or too sick. And whatever happens, we've got to look to the future. Supposin' we don't come back; supposin' we're all killed. We've got to think—'

'Yes, yes, I see what you're sayin',' croaked Doc, wiping a hand over his tired face. 'We go with what we've got.' He nodded and pushed through the 'wings to the crowded saloon bar.

'You want to take that old buffalo piece of mine, Doc?' called the old-timer. 'You're more than welcome.'

'We'll cope well enough,' smiled Doc. 'But thanks.' He gazed round the smoke-hazed bar at the anxious faces. 'Time's pressin',' he said quietly. 'There are folk waitin' on us, trustin' to us, so we'd best be makin' it to that desert trail.'

A bar girl sniffed back her sobs and dabbed at trickling tears.

Jay Matlan lit a fat cigar and gazed with a look of despair at the empty bottles, broken glasses and mess left by Quantril and his men.

'Any news of Eli?' asked a man at the bar.

'Too early,' said Wheeler, joining Doc. 'Don't expect him to make contact with anybody ridin' out of Gentry 'til sun-up. If then. We shouldn't be settin' too much store by it.'

'What about Sheriff Connell?' grunted the old-timer. 'Talk is he's followin' some Indian trail out there in the hills. That a fact?'

'That's a fact,' said Doc. 'But again, we're gamblin', just takin' a chance and hopin' we might get lucky. If the sheriff makes it to the border ahead of Quantril—'

'Goddamnit, we should've gotten a whole sight more difficult while we had them scum here in town,' growled the old man. 'Should've shot it up with them or somethin'.'

'And then spent God knows how long shovellin' dirt on Boot Hill while we buried the dead,' said the blacksmith, adjusting his gunbelt.

'That's right,' added Matlan from a cloud of cigar smoke. 'We did the best we could, and let's remember – Jake and Jessie are still breathin'.'

'As far as we know where Jessie's concerned,' said a man in the shadows. 'She sure as hell looked in a poor way when she left here. And then there's Abigail. . . .'

A sullen silence fell across the bar, broken only by the exaggerated tick of the clock, the quiet sniffs and snivels of the girls, and then, in a tone of bitter hatred, by the old-timer.

'Go get 'em, Doc. Get 'em for Bandyrock, for us, for Martha Wardman, Cord Chappell, Harry Macks. Get 'em and don't show no mercy.'

Connell heard the noise seconds before he saw the movement. He reined the mare to a halt instinctively. 'Steady, gal, steady,' he whispered, at the same time peering ahead through the thinning gloom of night to the sprawl of brush and rocks.

A bird about to clatter into dawn life? A hunting animal stalking its prey? A person, somebody out there watching him, tracking him?

Not one of the Quantril gang this deep into the Bluespecks, he figured. He sat easy, his concentrated gaze lifting briefly from the brush to the ranges ahead of him. No mistaking Sky Point towering through the surrounding crags like a giant hand reaching for the clouds. An hour's ride to the lower reaches, he decided. Given any luck, he would find the old hunting-trail and be following it long before noon.

Silence. No movements in the scrub. He patted the mare's neck and urged her forward.

The night would have lifted completely within the next two hours, he reckoned, his thoughts shifting again to the town, the posse Doc and Wheeler would be putting together, to Eli tracking way behind him, Jessie and Abigail, the chill of the desert beginning to fade to a new warmth and then a heat that would fry.

He grunted softly to his thoughts, gave the brush one last close look and flicked the reins for the mare to quicken the pace.

They left town with the few lights still burning, the shadows thick and heavy and the watching faces on the boardwalks, at windows, in doorways, grey with the anxiety and uncertainty of the hours to come.

Doc Merry led the posse with the simple order: 'We stay close, awake, and we don't miss nothin'. There's no sayin' to Quantril's exact route to the border, or the tactics he'll use to get there. Best we can do is not give him an edge. Keep it tight. If we can come to within a half-mile or so of his party, that'll do 'til we either meet up with Sheriff Connell or we get some support from somewhere.'

'And amen to that,' the blacksmith had quipped as the riders pulled out.

Bernard Wheeler wondered if he would ever see his mercantile again. The business had been his life, still was; worth fighting for to the last, he had resolved.

There would be a whole day of free drinks for all at the Split Spurs saloon if he came out of this alive, Jay Matlan had decided. A day of celebration for Bandyrock.

But that had seemed a world away as they followed

the trail out of town to the fringes of scrub, brush and scattered outcrops and eventually hit the sand. Nobody risked a last look back to the shapes among the fading lights. Nobody wanted, or needed, to be reminded of what they were leaving behind. The hope lay in seeing it again in the clear light of another day.

They were some hours into the ride, with the first hint of a pale light in the eastern skies, when Skip Marks, the youngest of the town posse, reined his mount alongside Doc Merry and held to his pace.

'See that low break of rocks way out to your left there, Doc? Well, I've been keepin' an eye on it, and two spits to a polished boot if I ain't seen some sort of light there, or mebbe somethin' glintin'.'

'Movin'?' asked Doc, swaying to the stride of his mount.

'Sometimes dead ahead, sometimes a touch to the right. It don't stay still that's for sure.'

'So what's your reckonin'?'

The young man pondered for a moment. 'My guess would be for it bein' one of Quantril's men. Could be he's decided to have somebody hang back to watch for who's followin'.'

'Could be,' agreed Doc. 'He'll want to know the strength of the trailin' posse and its distance from him. Crossin' that border is goin' to call for critical timin'.' They rode on for a while, Doc's gaze narrowing on the strengthening new light. 'You figurin' we should take a closer look?' he asked some minutes later.

'Mite risky if we all swing out to the rocks,' said Wheeler, his mount's pace steady at Doc's side.

The young man pulled at the brim of his hat. 'What say Art Toyne and me ride clear while the light's still spooky? Just take a look. The more we know about Quantril's plannin' and thinkin', the better chance we have of spikin' him when the time comes.'

Hoofs pounded to the sand, tack jangled, leather creaked, and the light began to spread like a slow stain.

'Go easy,' warned Doc. 'We're within a spit of treadin' on Quantril's toes. Don't let's spoil it.'

Jason Stock spat into the rocks at the outcrop, blinked on the shift of the light from night to day, and cursed quietly to himself.

Short straw. He had drawn the short straw in Quantril's decision to leave somebody trailing behind for a sight of any posse. And not for the first time, he grunted to his musings. This was Quantril's way of showing him who was boss – and his spiteful means of keeping him away from that homestead girl.

Well, Luke Quantril might be laughing into his stubble right now, but there would come a time – and you could bet to it – when things would change. The minute they crossed that southern border, the girl and the money owing him would be his and Quantril, Prof, the whole lot of them, could go to hell.

He would ride on deeper, way down into Mexican country, and when he tired of the girl he would trade her for one of them dark-eyed Spanish beauties. And then . . .

He blinked again on the shifting light. Now what in the name of . . . Two riders moving in from the left.

Town men, sure to be. Must have split from the main posse trailing out of Bandyrock. He grinned softly and drew his glinting Winchester to his side. This could be amusing, he reckoned. A real turkey-shoot to start the day.

Then he would dump the bodies right under Quantril's nose!

NINETEEN

Skip Marks glanced quickly at his partner through the veils of dawn light and swirls of desert dust and motioned for him to stay low to his mount's neck. Art Toyne was a willing rider to the posse, and a fair shot when he had a mind, but he sure as hell had a reckless streak. Get to it and think later, was Art's philosophy.

Skip flicked the reins for his mount to hold the pace and narrowed his gaze on the outcrop. Nothing glinting there now, he noted, but that was hardly surprising. If there was somebody out there, one of Quantril's men on the look-out for tracking riders, then he had surely spotted the approaching dust-cloud and deduced that he was soon to have company.

Skip spat gritty dirt from his mouth and glanced again at his partner. 'The rocks are higher and the shadows thicker to the left,' he called against the pound of hoofs and rush of air. 'We'll make for them at the last minute. Meantime, ride straight. Fool whoever's there into figurin' for us holdin' a direct line.'

Art signalled his understanding and settled to the

thudding rhythm, his eyes blinking furiously against the stinging dust and dirt. He gritted his teeth and focused best he could on the rocks ahead. No sign of a presence, he thought; no movements, nothing glinting or gleaming, but that was not to say the fellow had backed off. He would be waiting, judging the distance to a steady, levelled shot, and when it came . . .

It shattered the dawn like a spitting rage.

Skip's head filled with the blaze until it seemed it would split. He fell lower to his horse's neck, his hands suddenly tensed and wet on the reins, his eyes glazed as he watched a shower of blood spray like fire sparks from Art Toyne's chest.

'Hold on!' he yelled above the crashing roar of a second shot. 'Head to the left, f'cris'sake.'

But too late. Art was already sliding, as slow as a dead weight from the saddle, his mount snorting, wild eyes flashing on the strengthening light, hoofs spiralling ever thicker dust clouds as the horse raced out of control, dragging the lifeless body of Art in its wake.

Skip cursed, spat, blinked on water-filled eyes and urged his mount on until, like a mouth opening to swallow him, he reached the deeper shadows skidded the horse to a lathered halt, grabbed his rifle from its scabbard and plunged from the saddle to the rocks.

It was a full two minutes before Skip could see straight, feel the strength of his fingers on the weapon and gather something of his senses.

What the hell-fire had happened? Art was dead, shot clean through on that first blaze, nothing of him or his horse to be seen now.

He shivered at the sound of a spill of loose rocks somewhere deeper in the outcrop. His fingers tightened on the Winchester; blood pounded in his head as his anger rose. 'Sonofa-goddamn-bitch,' he mouthed on a hiss.

He cleared the sweat from his face and eased forward on his hands and knees, dragging the rifle with him. The light began to shimmer on the first of the rising sun. Shadows flitted, some to disappear completely, some to deepen for a moment as if taking a last breath.

Skip paused, waited, listened. The snort of a horse, stamp of a hoof into sand. Then silence.

He swallowed, crawled on a few more yards to the shelter of a larger, thicker boulder and paused again, suddenly chilled at the cold creep of sweat, 'Hell!' he cursed, but froze instantly at the lift and growing depth of the shadow of a man looming in front of him.

Skip had struggled to a kneeling position, grabbed the rifle to his hip and loosed a roar of shots almost before he was aware of the shattering sound and the haunting echo that filled the outcrop like the wailing of a ghost.

Doc Merry groaned inwardly with the effort of helping to lift Skip Marks to his horse and settle him in the saddle. 'Go easy,' he croaked. 'You're lucky to be alive. You've got a nasty wound there in the thigh, but you ain't goin' to come to a deal of harm if you keep it clean and rest up. I'll look to you the minute we get back.'

'And there's no sayin' when that might be,' added Jay Matlan gloomily as he chewed on an unlit cigar.

'We've got enough problems without addin' pessimism to 'em,' snapped Wheeler, shielding his eyes against the glare. He scanned the empty desert slowly. 'Nothin', he murmured. 'Not so much as a miserable buzzard.'

'Which is mebbe no bad thing,' said Levens, lifting his hat against the spread of sweat. 'Probably proves my reckonin' that the horse has headed back to town, and mebbe still trailin' Art's body.' He grunted. 'Hell, ain't that just goin' to be some encouragement to the folk left in town! All they need to see!'

'My doin', damn it,' winced Skip. 'Just didn't see a thing 'til it was too late. Sonofabitch must've been watchin' like a hawk.'

'No recriminations, there ain't the time,' said Doc. 'We know now that Quantril left that fella Stock behind as the look-out, so bein' followed is fixed in his reckonin'. What we also know, o' course, is that Stock's mebbe carryin' a wound as a result of Skip's shot. There's enough blood hereabouts, and it ain't all one man's.'

'Won't slow Quantril up,' said Wheeler, still scanning the desert. 'My bettin's on him layin' up another trap to spring on us.'

'That's for a fact,' agreed Doc, 'so we go extra careful. Eyes wide open; don't miss a thing.' He turned to Skip. 'Get yourself back to town, young fella. You did your best, but there's nothin' more you can do out here. You'll only hold us up at the pace you're goin' to have to ride.'

Skip nodded and reined his mount from the outcrop to the sand. 'You fellas take care, all right? And when you get to Stock, settle him for Art and me. Don't let the rat breathe another day.'

They watched the man ride out until he was lost in a swirl of dust.

'We mount up and move on,' ordered Doc, glancing quickly at the blood-smeared rocks and sand and wondering what manner of omen he might read into them had he a mind to linger.

'Due south!' he called, pointing the way.

Sheriff Connell had remained motionless for nearly ten minutes, his senses alive and alert to every sound however close, no matter how distant.

He had heard what he was certain now had been the whining echoes of rifle shots many miles away. Quantril's men? he had wondered; Doc Merry's pursuing posse out of Bandyrock? Or had Eli struck lucky and crossed riders trailing through the Bluespecks? The echoes had flared and died to leave the morning a half mile short of the peaks of Sky Point to its silent loneliness.

He came slowly from his squatting position low in the scrub, patted the black mare's neck and climbed carefully back to the saddle. He shielded his eyes against the spread of the glare and urged the mount forward at an even pace.

The next two hours of new light with the sun high in a cloudless sky would be crucial to the discovery of the old Navajo trail round the Point, he had pondered. No matter how fast Quantril might be making good his escape, and irrespective of the progress of the pursuing posses, finding that Indian trail and holding to it to the desert would determine the fates of more than Jessie Wardman and Abigail.

A town's future lay in the balance; men's lives were still at stake and more might yet come to die in Luke Quantril's bid for the southern border.

Connell pushed on through the glare, his gaze tight and concentrated on making a path for himself through the unrelenting scrub and brush, the mare snorting and tossing her head against the burrs and barbed growth attacking her chest and flanks.

The two hours had passed in a haze of heat and sweat and disappointment when Connell reined to a halt, peered closer at the tangles of scrub, and grunted quietly to himself. It was there – the track, vague and wickedly overgrown, but there.

He smiled. He could almost hear the soft padding of Navajo feet as they went to the hunt.

TWENTY

Quantril scuffed the toe of a boot through the sand and dirt, turned his back on the eyes watching him and took a quiet half-dozen steps into the burning glare of the high sun. It was a full minute before he spoke.

'You should've killed the pair of 'em. How come you didn't finish the job? You gettin' soft or somethin'?'

Jason Stock leaned heavily against the flank of his mount, his breathing tight and wheezing, his face glistening in a lather of sweat.

'In case it's escaped your notice, I'm bleedin' like a pig here,' he mouthed through a grating croak. 'That sonofabitch town lad got lucky with a loose shot, otherwise—'

'Yeah, yeah, I know,' interrupted Quantril impatiently. 'Otherwise he'd be eatin' desert dirt, that what you're tryin' to tell me?' He turned, his stare glazed and angry. 'Goin' to slow us down some, ain't it?'

'Well, I don't see . . .' began Stock, only to fall silent again under the stare, the tense awareness of the others.

Abigail glanced anxiously at Jessie where she sat her mount without seeming to breathe or blink. Prof adjusted his derby with an exaggerated fidget. Rimms McCane sniffed and examined his blackened finger-nails with concentrated interest. Charlie Loome shifted his weight from hip to hip and turned his eagle gaze to the distant horizon as if expecting to see it fill with bodies.

'You need a doc,' said Quantril, watching Stock dabbing at his shoulder wound with an already blood-soaked bandanna. 'And a doc we ain't got,' he added cynically. 'Leastways, save the one trailin' us, and I ain't for waitin' on him.'

'You ain't goin' to have to wait on nobody,' winced Stock. 'Get myself patched up minute we cross that border.'

Prof cleared his throat pointedly. 'Them southern dirt towns don't go much on doctorin',' he said almost lightly.

'I hear as how the sick just crawl away to die. Ain't much else for it,' chipped Loome, still scanning the horizon.

Abigail stiffened under a sudden chill. Rimms McCane blew on the tips of his fingers.

'Just talk,' groaned Stock. 'I'll find a doc, don't you fret. Let's just get ridin', eh? Time ain't standin' still, and I don't figure for that town posse bein' too far behind.'

Quantril scuffed a boot again. 'That's the whole point, ain't it?' he said carefully. 'That town posse catchin' up and, let's face it, friend, you not bein' in the best of condition and no real prospect of decent

116

doctorin'. Makes for a problem, don't it?'

'I don't see no problem,' grinned Stock through another wince and beading of sweat. 'All we got to do—'

'I know precisely what we've got to do,' said Quantril, his eyes wide, the stare darkening. 'We don't burden ourselves. We ride hard and them who can't stay the pace . . .'

He had drawn a Colt and blazed two fast shots before Stock had stopped to blink through his sweat.

'Now we can ride,' grinned Prof, with a satisfied sigh.

'See what I mean?' grinned McCane, shortening the rope to Abigail's mount as he drew her closer to him. 'Quantril don't mess none. But then you'd know that, you and him goin' back some like you do.'

Abigail tossed her loose hair and rode easy to the roll of the mount. 'Quantril's a rat,' she snapped above the beat of hoofs, 'and I don't give a damn who hears me say so. Kills his own as if they're trash.' She glanced quickly at the sidekick. 'You should watch your back there, mister. You could be next.'

McCane spat across the swirling dust. 'You should be watchin' your own, lady,' he smiled. 'No sayin' as to what the man's got planned for you. 'T'ain't goin' to be no picnic that's for sure.'

Abigail stiffened. 'I'll take my chances like I always have, but somebody's goin' to hang for the treatment handed out to the young girl. If you'll take my advice, you'll keep your hands off her.'

McCane's smile widened. 'You ain't in no position

for handin' out advice to nobody, lady. Your fate's clear as the sky up there: across the border, then deeper south, and when Quantril's all through with you he'll deal you out in some two-bit poker game. And I shan't be around to see none of it. Nossir. I'll be long gone.'

'And that's about the truest word you've ever said,' scoffed Abigail, 'You don't get around much when you're dead!'

Quantril called for a faster pace. 'We'll ease up again at Snake Creek,' he called. 'Just keep them females movin' or I might have to reconsider their prospects. Understand?' He flicked the reins. 'I ain't necessarily for leavin' dead bodies clutterin' this trail, but don't figure I won't if needs be.'

Abigail looked back through the shimmer of the dust cloud to where Charlie Loome trailed Jessie's mount close by him. The girl had barely flinched at the shooting of Jason Stock. She had simply blinked and continued to stare ahead, her body and senses immune, it seemed, to the forces around her. Now she rode easy again and in total silence.

Not for the first time since the light had lifted Abigail wondered just how much longer the girl could find the will to live with such tortured thoughts and images.

She sighed and dismissed the stab of pain in her spine, her gaze concentrating on the distant blur of the foothills to the Bluespecks. Were there eyes already watching from somewhere in the sun-baked rocks? Was there a posse trailing the remote tracks, or did the only hope rest with Doc Merry and the town men?

The certainty was that nothing would persuade Quantril against his bid for the southern border. He would kill first – as Stock had been so brutally reminded all too late.

Connell stoppered his canteen with a defiant thud, wiped the dribbles of water from his chin and narrowed his already concentrated gaze on the terrain ahead.

Not good, he decided, on a quiet grunt to himself. It would be tough going through the tangled scrub and along the tortuous track for some miles yet, but the old Navajo trail had remained true to the original map, skirting the higher reaches of Sky Point like a necklace. If he held to the pace, he thought, shielding his eyes against the glare as he scanned the sky, he would be through the worst and beginning to drop towards the desert again before the night closed in and darkness settled.

He patted the mare's neck, murmured his encouragement and urged her forward, his tall shadow drifting across the scrub and rocks as if in low flight. He listened intently for a moment, his mind spinning through the fantasy that he might pick up the beat of distant hoofs, the call of Doc Merry's party, the familiar voice of Eli. Or perhaps, more likely, the threat of Quantril.

He shook his head and dismissed his thoughts. There was nobody out here, nobody for at least twenty miles. But somewhere there was Jessie Wardman, Abigail and a town posse with almost no experience of trailing fast guns.

119

He clicked his tongue for the mare to find her steps through the scrub, watched the swirl of a hunting hawk high above him and went back to his concentration.

Quantril rode his party into Snake Creek with the last of the day's sun blazing its finale in the west.

'We'll rest up for an hour or so, no more,' he announced, slipping from his saddle. 'Prof here figures we're two, mebbe three hours ahead of the town posse. It'll be full dark by the time they reach here, but we'll be gone. We ride through the night for as long as we can, so make the most of the rest.'

He loose-hitched his mount in the shaded cool of the rocks and dusted the sand and dirt from his clothes. 'Look to that gal, Abigail, and no messin'. Rimms, you keep an eye on the pair of 'em.' He grunted before adding. 'And I mean an eye.'

Abigail had led Jessie to a sheltered stretch of the creek stream and helped her best she could to wash and ease the throb of her bruising and grazes. Little in the way of coherent words had passed between them, Jessie's eyes and attention being more concerned with the staring McCane than with Abigail.

'Take no notice of him,' Abigail had urged. 'He ain't worth nothin'. And don't you fret none, they'll all come to grief sooner or later.'

But the words had seemed to pass over the girl as if on the drift of the gathering evening breeze. Her gaze had clouded again, too vague and lost for even the tears to show, and Abigail had had no choice but to settle her quietly and as far away from Quantril, Prof and Charlie Loome as possible.

It was not until she had refreshed herself that McCane had approached through the deepening shadows. 'I got a proposition,' he murmured, watchful of Quantril's occasional glances. 'A near watertight guarantee that might just get you, me and the gal across that border alive.'

'You having second thoughts about your so-called partners?' Abigail hissed, her eyes narrowing tightly. 'I ain't got a spit of a reason to trust you, McCane, and I ain't seen nothing of late to change my mind.'

'Mebbe so, but like I said before, lady, you ain't in no position to make any choices over anythin'. My guess right now is that you'll listen up to whatever comes your way if it means survival.' McCane's grin had flitted across his face like light. 'You listenin'?'

TWENTY-ONE

Circling buzzards in the far distance had been the first indication to the town posse of dead meat ahead.

'One down; four rats to snatch,' Wheeler had muttered darkly once Doc Merry had made an examination of the blood-soaked remains of Jason Stock.

'And shot like the rat he was by the look of it,' Matlan had added to a chorus of grunts from the others.

'Quantril had reckoned him a burden,' said Levens. 'So that's what you get when a fella's desperate enough to escape the law. Don't say much for the others' chances.' He had stared at the body for some seconds before murmuring: 'Makes you wonder just how many are goin' to get a sight of that border. Mebbe Quantril and Prof are plannin' on keepin' the money for themselves.'

Matlan had stifled a shiver in spite of the evening heat. 'And that ain't sayin' nothin' for Jessie's and Abigail's chances,' he had grunted. The men had sat their mounts in thoughtful silence for a while, their gazes moving slowly across the empty land where the few shadows were already under threat as the light faded and night shuffled in.

'He'll ride for as long as he's able,' Doc had said, turning away from the body. 'He'll have reached Snake Creek by now, where he'll water up and mebbe rest an hour or so, then he'll hit the trail again and plan on coverin' all the ground he can make while he can – which don't leave us with no options, does it?'

By common consent they had left the buzzards to do their worst.

The light had retreated at last through a flaming dusk to the onset of night when Sheriff Connell turned his back on the darkening bulk of Sky Point and reined the mare into the face of the cooler breeze.

He reckoned for being a nose ahead of his planned progress to clear the scrub and rocks and pick up the trail to the border before full dark. If the moon rose bright and round and the cloud cover stayed high he would continue to ride for as long as he dared risk the black mare's willingness. She had been game enough through the heat of the day but would tire naturally as the night deepened, and he needed her as fresh as possible for the shadowless desert trails.

He steadied the pace, his hands easy on the reins, and peered carefully ahead. The track was beginning to drop to the clearer ground of looser rocks and shale-scattered drifts between boulders. He would need to go quietly, keeping the noise to a minimum as it travelled like echoes on the thin night air. Quantril and his men would be alive to every sound, every shift of shadow and movement.

But would they choose to ride on through the night, or keep their mounts fresh for the push to the border? Had the burden of their hostages slowed them down? How close had the town posse managed to get?

Connell swallowed deeply on his parched throat. Too many questions, too few answers. He eased the mount across a sharper slope, halted once the mare had clambered to a safer footing and peered intently ahead to where the rougher ground was lost in a cluster of boulders. Beyond them, thought the sheriff, lay the last of the thin scrub before the sand took over and the desert reached almost unbroken to the southern border.

He was lily-livered scared, or desperate, or mad, or perhaps suffering equal measures of all three if the truth were known.

Abigail licked her sun-dried lips, rolled to the steady pace of her mount and gazed carefully through the darkness to the riders ahead of her; more particularly the back of Rimms McCane.

She had listened to his hurriedly sketched proposition without interruption and one eye still on the hovering closeness of Quantril while the party had watered and rested up among the eerie shadows at Snake Creek.

'I ain't for messin', lady,' he had whispered, making an elaborate pretence of cleaning and replenishing his canteen. 'You've seen the way things are with Quantril, and I wouldn't for a spit figure for you not havin' the full measure of him and Prof. They're reck-

124

onin' on their own end to all this. Well, that ain't the way I'm seein' or plannin' it.'

McCane had waited, glanced round him, wiped a beading of sweat from his face, and continued: 'You stay as close as you can to that gal and do exactly what I tell you once we near that border. You don't question nothin'. Just do as I say when I say it – and don't take no notice of Charlie Loome. He's as two-faced as a double-head rattler. Do like I say and we'll all three stay alive.'

'And then?' Abigail had asked. 'What do we do when you've pulled off this remarkable escape?'

McCane's stare had retreated as if into shadow. 'You stay breathin', lady, and that's as good as it gets right now,' he had hissed. 'Choice is yours.'

But had she made it, she wondered, her own stare darkening as the riders pounded on through the night? When did McCane plan his move, where and how? Would Jessie be able to respond to any bid to escape? And just how far could she trust McCane, if at all, to keep his word?

But Abigail's thoughts were lost in the sudden yell from Quantril as Loome broke free from the party and reined his mount hell for leather into the depths of the night.

'Let him go!' boomed Prof as the party came to a dust-swirling halt and Loome raced on. 'He makes his own bed from here on. Sonofabitch!'

The horses snorted and stamped, their eyes wild and white as stars. Quantril grabbed the reins of Jessie's mount. 'He weren't goin' no place anyhow,' he growled.

'And what's that supposed to mean?' croaked McCane, spitting dirt from his parched mouth.

'He means Charlie was all washed up,' said Prof. The night breeze caught at the folds of his bandanna. 'That gut of his weren't gettin' him nowhere. I ain't fussed one bit about the rat. If he wants to go it alone to the border, so be it. I couldn't give a damn.'

Quantril growled his agreement. Abigail shivered, glanced anxiously at Jessie, then at McCane.

'Gettin' fewer, aren't we?' quipped the gunslinger, his eyes narrowing. 'Goin' to have to revise that bookkeepin' of yours, Prof. Looks like we might have a new deal on the table, eh?'

Prof adjusted the set of his derby, then wiped the back of his hand across his mouth. 'We'll get to that at the border, not before.'

McCane's face gleamed with a tight cynical grin. 'You bet we will. You bet.'

Abigail shivered again as Quantril ordered the party to move on. Nobody gave another thought to the disappearance of Charlie Loome. The night, it seemed, had claimed him. Or he had found it.

The suddenly pricked ears and gentle snort of the black mare alerted Connell to the faint noise far beyond his cover in the rough outcrop. He calmed the mount and eased himself from the depths of the darkness to make out whatever he could of the shapes in the night.

Nothing that was moving, he thought, but there was a noise, a dull monotonous thudding, that could mean only one thing: approaching riders. Quantril and his party, the town posse? Neither, he figured, his gaze tightening as he probed the shadowy forms, moonlit patches and desert emptiness beyond the scrub and rocks. Quantril could not have made this distance holding to the desert trail in this time; Doc Merry's town posse would be further back, and there had been no hint of Eli having made contact.

So, he pondered, who might be out here and heading at a pace on what seemed at the moment to be a course due west towards the Bluespecks?

He led the mare gently from the cover to the scrub, the loose rein secure in his hand, his steps measured and soft, senses alive to the gathering sound the slightest movement.

He halted after twenty yards, waited, listening, patted the mare's neck as her ears pricked again. He moved on, certain now that the rider was intent on reaching the thicker brush of the low hills that flanked the peaks and mountain ranges. But to do what, he wondered: hide, ride on to the west, keep a meeting, escape?

The sound deepened as the rider drew closer. Connell halted again, this time in the deeper shadow cast from an outcrop of boulders. His gaze narrowed. He saw a shape, the rider, low in the saddle, urging his wild-eyed mount to hold the hectic pace.

Another half-minute and he had a clear view of the man's face as he raced his horse through a patch of moonlight.

Charlie Loome!

Connell mounted up quietly and hesitated only seconds before reining to follow the shadowy rider.

TWENTY-TWO

It was a full fifteen minutes before the sound faded and the shape of the rider was lost in the thicker scrub and rocks flanking the Bluespecks.

Sheriff Connell slowed the black mare instantly to the slim cover of a clutch of boulders, and waited, listening, watching. Why had Loome split from the main party? Had he taken his share of the spoils, or had he been in dispute with Quantril and simply ridden out? Was he planning on travelling alone? The questions buzzed through Connell's thoughts, but of more concern right now was why had Loome stopped and where was he holed up? Had he detected somebody following?

Connell dismounted, loose-hitched the mare, patted her neck and drew his Winchester slowly, softly from its scabbard. He eased away to the shadows, his steps certain, his body bent low against the shafts of moonlight that would silhouette him as a clear target.

Still no sounds, no movements. Nothing save the night and the shroud of its cover.

He slid into the safety of rocks, settled his grip on

the rifle and peered deep into the darkness. Loome had not gone on, he was sure of that; he had halted somewhere up ahead. And that meant only one thing: however pressing the time taken, he was not for being followed. He was making his journey alone.

Connell's gaze shifted to the left, concentrated, moved on, concentrated again. Nothing – but he was too late to react to the crunch of the step at his back.

'Ease that piece and your gunbelt to the dirt, mister, and raise your hands real slow.'

Charlie Loome's voice cut across the night like a steel blade scraped between rocks. Connell did as he was ordered, then came slowly upright raised his hands and stiffened.

'Well, now, hadn't figured for crossin' you again so soon,' said the sheriff, his senses tuned for every sound, the slightest movement. 'How come? You and Quantril been bad mouthin' each other?'

'None of your business,' snapped Loome. He was silent for a moment, the rasp of his breathing the only sound across the night. 'Stock's dead,' he announced bluntly. 'So's one of your town men. They had a shoot-out, but it was Quantril who killed Stock. He ain't for bein' trusted, not now he's only a spit short of the border and he's holdin' the money.'

A thin lather of sweat had beaded on Connell's brow at the news of the shootings. 'And the girls?' he asked hoarsely. 'They safe?'

'For now. Wouldn't rate their chances once they hit that border.'

Connell licked his lips. 'You figurin'—'

'Gettin' you off my back, lawman,' rasped Loome.

'Should've done it back there in Bandyrock, minute I reckoned for crossin' you in Kimberly.' He spat precisely. 'I ain't much for lawmen, specially when they get to followin'. Turn round.'

Connell turned slowly, conscious of Loome taking a step back to the deeper darkness. Their eyes met in an icy stare.

' 'T'ain't goin' to work, Charlie,' said the sheriff. 'You clear these hills and mountains, ride as far and wide as you like, some day they're goin' to find you and gun you down like a dog.' His eyes narrowed. 'Think about it.'

'I ain't for any thinkin' that concerns you. All the thinkin' you need to ponder on is comin' to rot out here in these god-forsaken hills.' The Colt, levelled in his hand, gleamed in a drift of the moonlight.

'Mebbe not so forsaken,' said Connell, his thoughts swirling in a bid to gain time against the blaze of Loome's gun.

'What you sayin'?'

Connell lowered his hands a fraction and licked his lips. 'I'm here, and ahead of you,' he said, his gaze tight on the gunslinger's face. 'How'd you figure that? And how do you know I'm alone? You don't.'

Loome spat again. 'You're alone,' he grinned. 'I ain't that dumb. As to how you got here, who gives a damn? Fact is, lawman, you're in my way, wastin' my time. And time I ain't for treatin' lightly, not right now I ain't when I got these hills to clear.'

'You won't make it,' croaked Connell. 'That I promise.'

'We'll see – leastways I will. You won't be around!'

Loome's grin twitched and deepened as his fingers eased for a new, firmer grip on the Colt.

The sheriff's hands lowered again, this time giving him the balance he needed for his one, and he guessed only, chance to save himself.

The toe of his right boot slid beneath a stone, kicked at it viciously and lifted the weight just high enough from the ground to send it crashing into Loome's ankle. The Colt blazed behind a growled curse, but the shot was already clearing Connell's shoulder as the sheriff launched himself like a swooping hawk into Loome's midriff.

They crashed to the dirt in a tangle of thrashing limbs, Connell fighting wildly to loosen the Colt from the gunslinger's grip. He crashed a clenched fist into Loome's cheek, winced as scrambling fingers tore at his throat like claws, then landed the fist in a second blow across a stubbled jaw.

Loome's eyes rolled; he frothed at the mouth, pulled himself clear, the Colt settling again in his hold.

'To hell with you!' seethed Connell through clenched teeth. The fist flew again, this time cracking across Loome's cheekbone with the sound of splintering wood.

The gunslinger groaned, the piece slipping from his fingers as if melting. Connell gasped, reached for the Winchester at his back and levelled it in a one-handed grip.

'Not so easy, lawman!' spat Loome, scrambling through the dirt and into the darkness of a maze of rocks and boulders.

Connell cursed, staggered to his feet and plunged forward. Loome had retrieved his Colt; he was armed again and desperate now to make good his getaway.

'Sonofabitch!' mouthed the sheriff as the first shot roared from the depths of the rocks. He slid to cover, the sweat dripping like rain from his face, his limbs throbbing. Listen, he thought, licking his lips, narrowing his eyes, just listen, sooner or later the man had to move.

Seconds drifted to minutes. Connell crouched motionless still waiting, listening for that tell-tale shift of a boot. The darkness began to show the first smudge of light in the east. It would be dawn in an hour. He drew the Winchester closer, released one hand and felt for the pebbles at his feet. The clatter of them as a handful fell from his throw echoed through the rocks as if ghosts were spitting teeth.

Connell rose slowly from his cover, tense, aching, a trickle of blood at his neck, his eyes burning through the eerie drift from dark to light. He swallowed. A shape grew slowly in the rocks, at first no more than a blur, then a darkness that thickened.

There was the clear shape of a hat, a head, a body as Loome made his bid to slip away; a moment when it seemed he might simply turn and scramble into the shadows like a spooked gopher. But he hesitated, intent on one last attempt to shoot the man he feared might sit on his tracks and haunt him.

And it was then, with the gleam of the Colt barrel clear in Connell's vision, that the sheriff's Winchester roared in its anger and threw the gunslinger back to the depths of the darkness in a suddenly groaning, twisted heap.

Connell waited a full minute before stepping carefully to where the body lay in its rocky grave. Loome's eyes were open wide, lifeless and staring into the Bluespecks where the smudges of first light were clearing the high, silent peaks.

Charlie Loome would see nothing of them this or any other day.

Doc Merry halted his tired, dust-streaked party a half-mile or so out of Snake Creek.

'Quantril ain't wastin' no time, that's for sure,' he announced, wiping the dust and dirt from his face. 'He's two, mebbe three hours ahead and movin' some.' He sighed, blinked on the gathering light of the new day and pocketed his sodden bandanna with a grunt. 'Fact is, fellas, unless them rats out there get held up somehow by somethin' or somebody, we ain't goin' to make it. These horses just ain't for it. Quantril's goin' to hit the border at least an hour before we get so much as a sight of it.'

'Hell,' groaned Wheeler, removing his coat and shaking it. 'Can't give up now, Doc. We've got to think of somethin', and fast.' He shook the coat again and wafted aside the cloud of dust.

Matlan rummaged for a half-smoked cigar and lit it. 'Could be the sheriff's made it through the hills. Or mebbe Eli's met up with a posse,' he said from behind a haze of smoke.

'Yeah, but that's all mebbes. Jessie and Abigail ain't goin' to stay breathin' on possibilities.'

'Mebbe there is a way,' said the blacksmith, pushing his rolled shirtsleeves over his arm muscles.

'Spit it out,' snapped Doc, his gaze scanning the horizon. 'Any suggestion's got to be better than standin' here.'

Levens looked round him for a moment, at the tired men, the weary horses, the gathering light that would soon clear the skies to their cloudless blue and the scorching sun.

'Two of us ride on, trailin' spare mounts,' he said flatly. 'Nothin' else for it. That way we hold to some sort of steady pace and have reasonably fresh mounts to switch to before we reach the border.'

'You mean two of us walk back to Snake Creek and simply wait?' frowned Wheeler. ' 'T'ain't the walkin' that's a problem, but the waitin'. Hell, that ain't goin' to be so easy. For instance, what—'

'No choice,' said Doc. 'What Adam says makes sense.'

'But two of you ain't goin' to stop Quantril,' said Matlan, blowing a line of smoke. 'We need all the guns we can muster at the border. Two ain't goin' to be nothin' like enough.'

'We'll be meetin' up with the sheriff, and mebbe Eli's got lucky.'

Wheeler grunted. 'We're back to mebbes again.'

'That's where we've always been,' murmured Doc. He slapped his thigh. 'But not from here on. Myself and Adam here ride on fast as we're able trailin' spares. What we find at the border is another matter we'll deal with when we get there. It's the gettin' there before Quantril crosses that's the priority.'

TWENTY-THREE

Prof raised an arm and waved it towards a lone bulge of rocks, little more than shade for two men and their mounts but all there was in the searing, sun-drenched desert. The riders moved to the outcrop, reined to a halt and reached instinctively for their canteens.

'Look to the women,' ordered Quantril, glaring at McCane. 'And go easy. We're goin' to need water some distance over the border.'

Abigail wiped the sweat from her face and neck as she gazed anxiously at Jessie. The girl was holding up but only by whatever dregs of will-power she was still able to summon. She might give up at any moment. God willing it would not be here. Abigail could imagine Quantril's reaction with his patience, temper and obsessive intent on reaching the border already vying like hungry rats.

She turned her attention to McCane. He had kept his distance during the ride following Loome's sudden disappearance, said nothing and stared fixedly ahead as if lost in a maze of his thoughts.

So had he abandoned his plan after Loome's

action, or would he still spring it once the moment was right? Here and now, up ahead, or at the border? She tensed as he approached and offered the canteen.

'Stay close, stay ready,' he murmured.

Abigail drank gratefully. 'How you going to get the girl now that Quantril's trailing her?' she whispered, returning the canteen.

'Mebbe I ain't.'

'That ain't in the deal,' hissed Abigail.

'There ain't no deal, lady. I hold the cards and I play the game. Just do as I say.'

She reined her mount round at the snap of Quantril's voice.

'Last push to the border. Same pace, no stoppin', not for nothin'. You happen to see anythin', you still keep goin'. You understand what I'm sayin', lady?' His glare fixed on Abigail like a beam.

'I understand perfectly well,' said Abigail, stiffening as she tossed her hair. 'All I want to know—'

'Don't waste your breath,' grunted Prof. 'Save it. You're mebbe goin' to need it.' He grinned as he tapped the top of the derby. 'I said mebbe.'

Quantril closed on Jessie's mount, took the trail line and led the horse away. 'You look to the bar whore there, Rimms,' he called, 'and don't let her fool you none. She's a rattler as I recall. But we'll get to her later. Meantime—'

'Hold on there,' clipped McCane, his gaze tight and narrowed on Quantril and Prof. 'Ain't we got somethin' to settle?'

Quantril turned, his face taut and dark. Prof wiped the sweat from his neck. Abigail stiffened again. Was this to be the moment?

'Settle?' frowned Quantril. 'Now what would that be?'

'Save the stallin', Luke. You know well enough what I'm talkin' about.' McCane had released his hold on the line to Abigail's mount and his hand was at his side – within a whisker of his holstered Colt. 'I'm referrin' to them spoils we took out of Bandyrock. The money. More specifically, my share of it.' The fingers of the loose hand flexed and stretched. 'I figure I should be knowin' how much now that we're down to just the three of us.'

Prof coughed, brushed a fly from his sweat-streaked cheek and said: 'Are you sayin', Rimms, as how you want me right now, at this precise moment with us still short of the border by some miles and a town posse I imagine still high-tailin' us, to start countin' out a bag full of money just so's you can have the satisfaction of gloatin' over how much you've got comin'?' He brushed at the same persistent fly. 'That it?'

'That's it,' grunted McCane, the fingers still, the gaze steady. ' 'Ceptin' for one thing.'

'That bein'?' asked Prof.

'That I get my share now. Right here. Every last dollar due.'

Abigail glanced quickly from McCane, to Prof, to Quantril, the dazzling sun, the pestering flies, the restive horses. Would McCane go for his gun, she wondered? Perhaps more to the point, would Quantril? And who would draw first?

'Right now, right here . . .' echoed Prof. He settled the derby again. 'Well now, I judge from that, Rimms, that you're plannin' on pullin' out before we reach the border? That the way of it?'

'What I'm plannin' ain't no business of yours.'

'Oh, but I think it is. Very definitely. You see, Luke and me are kinda keen on knowin' just who's where and what they might or might not be doin' – or sayin', if you get my meanin'.' Prof's grin flittered loose and wet at his lips. 'Now, we know well enough to Stock, and Charlie ain't got no future with that gut of his. But you, my friend, are a different matter.'

Quantril's mount shifted restlessly. The sounds of creaking leather, tinkling tack seemed to fill the morning. McCane's fingers flexed again. Abigail swallowed on a parched throat.

'Luke and me got a future,' continued Prof. 'We don't want no law trouble as a result of loose talkin', do we? Mebbe it's best that we stick together, eh? Real friends, just like we've always been.'

McCane's Colt was drawn and levelled in an instant. 'Don't give me that,' he sneered. 'I've got the measure of this: you're figurin' on keepin' the money for yourselves. You ain't got no intention of a share-out, save between the pair of you. So I take my cut now. Get busy, Prof, before I reckon on takin' the lot.'

Abigail shuddered. Quantril spat.

Prof simply spread his wet grin. 'Gettin' anxious, aren't you. That ain't good, 'specially as we're wastin' time and givin' them posse rats all the chance they need to catch up. We don't want that, do we? So why—'

'No more stallin',' grated McCane, the sweat beginning to bead on his brow, his face to gleam as if lit from behind. He levelled and prodded the Colt. 'And while we're at it, you drop them weapons. All of 'em: sidearms, rifles. . . . Do it!'

Abigail's mouth opened, closed. She licked her lips, felt her hands turn sticky. Where was this going? How did McCane plan to ride clear? She glanced at Jessie who still sat her mount as if staring into a distance of her own vision. And what, wondered Abigail, of her fate?

She blinked and swallowed again as the weapons thudded to the sand under McCane's watchful gaze.

'You're makin' a big mistake here, Rimms,' croaked Quantril. 'It ain't goin' to work.'

'I'll be the judge of that,' clipped McCane. 'Just get on with it.'

Prof made a fussy gesture towards his saddlebag. 'I ain't able to start accountin' money seated up here,' he pronounced. 'I'm goin' to have to dismount, set about this cashin' up in a proper manner. Don't want no mistakes, not when it comes to hard-earned gains. You'd agree with that, Rimms. Sure you would.'

'Do it, real slow,' said McCane, the impatience and frustration glistening in his sweat. He turned to Abigail. 'Collect them weapons. Bring 'em to me.'

She dismounted, stepped carefully through the sand to the guns and gathered them up without a sound, her eyes deliberately averted from Quantril and Prof. Only when she had the butt of a Colt in her hand did she hesitate, suddenly mad enough to imagine that she might shoot her way to freeing Jessie and riding out to Doc Merry's town posse.

'Don't get no grand ideas, lady,' said McCane, as if

reading her thoughts. She tossed her hair and returned to the gunslinger.

'Might say the same of you, mister!' she hissed. 'How the hell are you goin' . . . She swung round at the sound of Prof's exaggerated cough.

'This ain't goin' to be easy,' he grunted, lifting a tied, bulging bag from his saddle. 'And it ain't goin' to be done in five minutes neither. You sure about all this, Rimms? Ain't there another way?'

'I could take that bag without the bother of you openin' it,' quipped McCane, prodding the Colt again. 'Sooner you get started, sooner we're through.'

'Sure, sure,' soothed Prof. 'Just like you say.'

Quantril sat his mount without moving, his face shadowed under the broad brim of his hat, his eyes gleaming, hands easy one atop the other. Jessie continued to stare without seeming to blink. Abigail licked her lips, sweated, shifted her feet anxiously. McCane simply watched, the Colt steady in his grip.

'Tell you somethin' for nothin',' said Prof, unwinding a length of cord from the neck of the bag. 'We made a fair haul back there in Bandyrock. As much as we've sometimes taken from a bank, and a darn sight easier! Know what, we could make a whole new profession of holdin' a town to ransom. Just imagine . . .'

Prof's right hand delved deep into the bag, his hidden fingers squirming in the dark like worms. McCane watched fascinated, the sweat beading on his face.

'Yeah,' murmured Prof, 'just imagine.' The fingers in the bag were suddenly still. A smile began to spread slow and wet at Prof's lips. 'But not for you, Rimms.

You just ain't goin' to be around.'

The shot from the gun inside the sack ripped through the fabric like flame, spilling coins and a fluttering of banknotes to the sand as McCane's eyes widened and his mouth dropped open. He slid from the mount as if his limbs had filled with water; the Colt slipped from his fingers, his hands clamouring at his gut in one last movement before he twitched into death.

Abigail staggered back, the chill of her shock consuming her. Quantril sighed, grinned and patted his mount's neck with quiet satisfaction.

'Tidy,' was all he murmured.

Prof withdrew his hand from the sack, the gun he had there still smoking in his hand, then stooped to collect the notes and coins from the sand.

'I ain't for throwin' money away,' he croaked to himself.

Abigail shuddered, conscious now of the weapons scattered in the sand around her, wondering again if she might make one decisive lunge to arm herself, get to Jessie's side. She glanced at the girl who had shown barely a reaction to the shooting. Her eyes flicked to Quantril, who simply smiled through his steady stare into her face.

'I can read you like a book, lady,' he croaked drily. 'You're figurin' to shoot your way out of this, eh? Just pick up one of them guns there and blaze away. Well, you know somethin', you wouldn't get a finger on the trigger.' His smile faded. 'So you stand right back. Now!' Abigail shuffled backwards, her hands wet and loose at her sides.

'Collect them guns, Prof, then we pull out. We take the girl, but the bar whore we leave.' Quantril sat upright in the saddle. 'She ain't of no further use and I ain't for bein' bothered with her once we've crossed the border. She ain't worth the effort.'

Abigail shuddered again, swallowed and squinted into the shimmering desert glare.

'We goin' to feed her to the buzzards along with Rimms here? She'd make a tasty dessert!' grinned Prof.

'Just leave her,' snapped Quantril, reining his mount to collect Jessie. 'The sun and heat will be a whole sight more painful. Let's ride. We've got time and distance to make up.' He stared hard into Abigail's eyes. 'You're gettin' off light, lady, just remember that. Another time, another place and you'd have been pleadin' for me to be this generous.'

It was a long three minutes before the riders and their hostage were a grey blur in a dust shroud and Abigail stood alone.

TWENTY-THREE

The slow mournful circling of buzzards had spurred Doc Merry and Adam Levens to a lathering pace as they closed on the outcrop of rocks. McCane's body was already infested with flies as the townsmen reined to a halt, dismounted and led their mounts to the narrow strip of shade.

'Hell,' mouthed Adam on the discovery of Abigail sprawled in the deepest of the shadow, her body pressed tight to the rocks. 'She alive, Doc?' he croaked, the sweat chilling in his neck.

'In poor shape, damn near exhausted, but she somehow got lucky, thank God. Hand me a canteen, then go look to the horses.'

'We takin' her with us?'

'Nothin' else for it. Can't leave her here.' Doc eased the woman's head to his lap where he squatted. 'But don't waste no time on the scumbag back there. The buzzards can have him.'

Adam pushed his hat from his forehead as he shielded his eyes against the glare and scanned the surroundings.

'So what happened here? Them rats beginnin' to fight among themselves?'

'Just that,' grimaced Doc. 'Thieves fallin' out, with Quantril and Prof takin' the spoils. My bettin' is there'll be just the two of 'em by the time they hit that border.'

'And young Jessie. What about her?'

Doc gazed deep into Abigail's face as her eyelids began to flutter and her lips to move under the cool of the water.

'That I don't know, Adam, and that's the truth. But I'm sure as hell prayin' the Good Lord's ridin' with her. Right now that's about her only hope.' He propped Abigail against the rock face. 'Ten minutes and she'll be fit enough to ride one of them spares.'

The two men waited in silence watched by the buzzards and pestered by the flies.

The sun was still high in a cloudless sky and the heat shimmered mercilessly across the desert sands and few scattered rocks as Quantril, Prof and Jessie made their steady way towards the southern border.

Jessie continued to ride in silence, her stare unblinking, grey and lifeless, her mind numbed to the pace, the sounds, the heat and the sight of her captors. She had seemed to flinch only once in her awareness that Abigail was being left behind at the outcrop, but the moment had been fleeting and passed in silent resignation. Now, she simply rode to Quantril's rhythm and bidding.

Prof's attention on the far horizon had been broken only by the occasional glance to left or right as the man squinted for recognition of some expected landmark. But not until he had urged Quantril to veer to the left and had ridden on for another half-mile did he eventually call to rein up.

'What we stoppin' for?' hissed Quantril, fluttering a bandanna before wiping it across his face. 'This somewhere special or somethin'?'

'Nowhere special,' said Prof, 'just that it's decision time again.'

'You mean we have choices in this god-forsaken hole? All I want is that border.'

'And you're goin' to get it,' smiled Prof, dusting the battered derby then settling it on his head again. 'But we do have options. One: we ride in a direct line for the border and cross it through open land. Or two: we continue to swing to the left and give ourselves the benefit of cover in the last of them Bluespecks foothills should we need it against any marauding posse. Question is, which? You have an opinion on the matter?'

Quantril spat, mopped his face again and squinted into the glare. 'I ain't fussed none,' he grunted drily. 'I don't reckon for any posse gettin' to us now, not if we keep movin'. Them town men are still some way behind. Charlie Loome's probably ridin' hell for leather into them goddamn mountains, and Stock and McCane are dead.' He grinned. 'That leaves you and me, Prof. And, o' course, the money. I figure for us havin' a clear run whichever way we go. So it's your choice. Do as you think fittin'.'

Prof fingered the battered brim of the derby. 'We play safe. We head for the cover and cross there.'

'Suit yourself,' shrugged Quantril.

'We keepin' the girl?'

'If we're playin' safe, we keep her 'til we've crossed.'

Prof nodded, pointed to the blurred line of the foothills to the left and reined his mount forward. The riders were lost in their own dust in less than a minute.

Sheriff Connell licked at an annoying trickle of sweat, squinted down the gleaming barrel of the Winchester and levelled his aim to within a fraction of dead centre of the man's head.

He could take out Luke Quantril with a single shot even at this distance. But he would wait, he decided, just long enough to be absolutely certain he did not miss. He relaxed where he sprawled in the clutch of rocks on the drift of the foothills a quarter-mile short of the border, and tightened his gaze on the approaching riders. Just three: Quantril, Prof and Jessie. Somebody's gun had been busy. But what of Abigail; what of the town posse?

He shifted to ease his legs, conscious that unanswered questions and the chilling doubts they raised only gnawed at his concentration. The shot was all that mattered. . . .

Quantril remained mounted as the blaze merely skimmed the flesh of a shoulder to raise no more than a stifled groan from the man and a deepening blood-stain across his shirt.

'Hell,' cursed Connell, quickly levelling the rifle for another attempt. But too late now. Prof and Quantril were already low to the necks of their mounts and racing for the rocky foothills to the sheriff's left. Jessie, more out of instinct than judgement, simply clung on and allowed her mount to be dragged between her two captors.

'Sonsofbitches!' cursed Connell again, wiping the sweat from his face in the frustration of realizing that a second shot might put the girl's life at risk.

He watched helpless as Quantril and Prof drew closer in a thickening cloud of dust to the cover of the rocks. He licked his lips, raised the Winchester to his shoulder, levelled the aim. One last shot while the rats were still in his sights. Fast, accurate.

He loosed the blaze and stared through a blurred gaze of sweat as Quantril was hurled headlong from his horse to the rocks.

'You messed it up, Prof, messed it up real good.' Quantril groaned, tightened his already blood-coated fingers on the wound at his shoulder, and hissed like a snake through clenched teeth. 'Now hand me that canteen, f'cris'sake, then get to doin' somethin' about the bullet I got buried in me.'

Prof moved quickly from mount to mount, settling them, hitching them, disregarding Quantril. He dragged the girl from her horse and bundled her roughly into cover, his cold stare enough to warn her not to move or call out.

It was a long three minutes before he was satisfied. He turned almost casually to face Quantril.

'Ain't you some sight,' he quipped behind a wet, dusty grin.

Quantril moaned and winced again, trying now to shift his body.

'Get that canteen, will you? And give me a hand here, f'cris'sake!'

Prof relaxed against a rock face. 'Is it worth it?' he sneered. 'I mean you ain't goin' no place, are you?'

'What the hell are you talkin' about?' Blood continued to seep through Quantril's fingers.

Prof adjusted his derby. 'You know who fired that shot?' he asked. 'Bet you can't guess.'

Quantril hissed and shuddered on a spasm of pain.

'Well, I'll tell you,' Prof said. 'That was Sheriff Connell, lawman at Bandyrock. Still is him. He's out there, waitin' on us. Just itchin' to fire another shot.'

'How'd you know that?'

'Figured it out,' smiled Prof, licking his lips. 'We ain't seen nothin' of him, have we, not since leavin' that two-bit town? Stock said nothin' about him. Why wasn't Connell leadin' that shoot-out? Got to be the town's best shot, ain't he? So where was he?' Prof pushed himself from the rock face. 'He weren't nowhere near that town posse. He was out there in them hills somehow managin' to get ahead of us.'

'You never said,' croaked Quantril.

' 'Course I didn't, but I knew he'd be here. Oh, yes, you bet I did.'

Quantril's face lathered in a glistening sweat, the dust and dirt as grey as craters, his eyes narrowed to slits, his lips twitching. 'You planned this,' he grated. 'Planned it all along.' He swallowed, winced, unaware of the steady trickle of blood through his fingers. 'Rode into these rocks on the gamble of Connell takin' a shot at me, didn't you? Sure you did. Now you're plannin' on finishin' it. You and the girl and

148

the money crossin' that border. Then you'll dump the girl, or kill her and . . . that's it! Then it'll be just you and the money. You sonofa-goddamn-bitch!'

Prof's smile widened. 'Say this for you, Luke, you sure click on quick. Ain't missed a trick there, savin' to say that you couldn't move even if you wanted – more to the point *if I* wanted you to – so I reckon for this bein' the end of the line.'

'Rat!' hissed Quantril, wincing again. 'Then you'd better get on with it. And fast. I ain't for keepin' your company a second longer than necessary.' He made an effort to spit, but managed only to groan and dribble.

Prof tapped the derby, dusted his coat and moved to the cover of the rocks to his right. 'I know you're out there, Connell,' he called, 'so you listen up real good. I'll say this once and once only. Quantril's about all through. You did a good job there. Nice shootin', but I'll finish it for you. Then me and the girl are pullin' out. Ridin' clear for that border we can both see. You know the deal: you make one move against me and the girl dies. Understand?'

The hot, shimmering day fell to silence again until, minutes later, a single shot broke it and echoed across the sand.

TWENTY-FIVE

Connell tensed, twitched at the crack of the shot, mouthed a curse, and squirmed clear of his cover in the rocks for the open ground behind him.

He came carefully to his feet, the Winchester tight in his grip, his shirt clinging to his back in a lathering of sweat. His gaze narrowed and fixed on the shimmering sprawl of rocks, sand and scrub around him. What now? Would Prof make a headlong dash for it, or would he head out slowly, using the girl as his cover? Would Jessie be up to it; what state was she in?

'You still out there, Sheriff?' called Prof.

'I'm here. I'm waitin' on you,' answered Connell as calmly as he could manage. 'You harm that girl in any way, and I swear to God—'.

'Yes, yes, I know all that,' grated Prof. 'Let's be realistic. I'm holdin' the aces, Connell, same as I've always done. But you don't get to play yet, if you follow my meanin', so you're goin' to have to content yourself with bein' a spectator. Get me?'

'I'm listenin',' replied Connell, already skulking away to the deeper cover.

'And no clever stuff. Whatever you're figurin', it won't work. It's just you and me out here. That town posse's still some way back – and remember, Connell, this girl here don't mean a thing to me. I'll shoot her as easy as spittin'. Bear that in mind, eh?'

'I shall,' called Connell, still moving quietly, silently through the rocks like an anxious insect, his eyes straining against the heat and shimmer for the slightest hint of a movement. 'You've got my word,' he croaked, catching at his breath. 'Just don't harm her.'

Silence. Connell halted, watching, waiting. 'Shift, damn you!' he hissed, swallowing on a dirt-dry throat. He heard the scuff of a hoof, a snort, the soft jangle of tack. Prof was saddling up. Another few minutes and he would be ready and moving out of the rocks.

Connell's stare settled like a beam on the heat haze. Could he risk a fast shot, he wondered? If he missed he might put the girl in greater danger, or spook Prof sufficiently to send him charging for the border in a swirling cloud of dust. No saying as to the fate of Jessie.

He crept on, still conscious of the snorts, the jangle of tack. He reached a thicker grouping of rocks, slid into them and risked a careful squirm over the baked surfaces to peer into the clearer spaces.

Prof was checking the fastening on his saddlebag, then tugging on the trail rope to Jessie's mount. The girl sat motionless, grey, silent, her stare seeing nothing. The flesh at her neck and exposed shoulders beneath what remained of the rags of her dress was bruised and scratched, the smears of blood dried and cracked like spots of red rain. She seemed emptied of all senses, a living thing somewhere between its last

151

breath and death.

Connell gulped and cursed quietly, the Winchester instantly alive in his grip. He could risk the shot from here. Shoot Prof clean between the shoulder blades. No chance he would miss, not at this distance. But he had never shot a man in the back. . . .

'You made it. Expected you sooner.'

Connell started at the suddenness of Prof's voice, the sweat beading like ice on his brow.

'Figured you'd risk it,' said Prof, without turning from his saddlebag. 'You're that sort of fella: a solid, upstandin' lawman just doin' his job.' He paused a moment. 'But not a very smart one.' He swung round from the saddlebag, a Colt already drawn and levelled in his grip on the girl. 'So you just drop whatever weapon you got there and ease out from them rocks real slow. And remember, nothin' clever. 'T'ain't fittin' in an upstandin' lawman!'

Connell let the Winchester clatter to the ground and stepped watchfully into the full glare. He had missed nothing of the irony and sarcasm in Prof's voice, and now he could see why. He squinted at the sprawled, dead body of Quantril, the flies gathering like a black cloud at his face, arms and hands; the staring, zombie-like figure of Jessie Wardman, remarkably statuesque on her tired, lathered mount, but a world apart, he thought, from the grim reality of the moment. And Prof – smiling now, the Colt still steady and deliberately aimed at the girl, his eyes gleaming.

'End of the line,' he grinned. 'Just like I told my good friend Luke there.' He took a deep breath. 'But let's not waste time, eh, Sheriff? Good lawmen do not waste time, as you've so effectively demonstrated. So here's the final deal.'

'You mean the last double-cross,' quipped Connell, his expression darkening.

'Have it your way. Merely a play on words.' Prof adjusted the derby with his free hand. 'You're goin' to start walkin' – and I mean walkin' – right here at my side, you on my left, the girl on my right. And when I figure for us bein' a spit and a bit close enough to that border, then I'll ride on, free as the wind. And you, Mr Connell, will be right there to watch me go. Mebbe I'll take the girl with me, mebbe not. We'll see. But should them town posse men show their faces, then I'll shoot you and the girl and take my chances. Ladies first, of course. What you reckon? Shall we go?'

The heat was unbearable, as searing as a flame, the air thick, unmoving, near suffocating as Connell fought for every breath in his trudge at the side of Prof's sweating mount.

He brushed at a pestering fly and glanced anxiously through his already blurred vision to focus on the girl mounted on the trailed horse to Prof's right. She was still as motionless, silent, lifeless as ever, her gaze unmoving on the shimmering haze ahead.

He swallowed, wiped a new surge of sweat from his face and let his senses drift back to the drone of Prof's voice.

'. . . now if Quantril were here, God rest his rottin' soul, he'd be all for makin' a hell for leather dash for it. Caution to the wind, never gave nothin' and nobody a thought – but that, you see, is where he'd

153

have been makin' his mistake.'

Connell hissed a soft curse as more sand worked its way into his boots.

'. . . big mistake. This way – should there be any eyes watchin', and you can bet your sweet life they're out there – this way I can be dead-set sure they ain't goin' to get within a drunk's spit of me.'

Connell's eyes clouded with sweat, his legs were leaden with the trudge through sand, his body aching.

'. . . they might risk takin' a shot, I hear you thinkin'. True, they might. But figure the consequences: one shot from out there and I'd kill the girl. 'Course I would. Only natural, ain't it?'

Connell blinked, clearing what he could of his vision to focus on the shimmering haze.

'. . . which is why, of course, they wouldn't risk it, 'specially not that Doc Merry. He's a thinkin' fella same as yourself. You wouldn't risk it, would you?'

Connell blinked again. A smudge, a definite shape beyond the shimmer. He could see it, not clearly but it was there.

'. . . you would not. And that's why, Mr Connell, I chose to do things this way. I'm a careful fella. Always have been. I think things through, same as I have since we pulled out of Bandyrock. I could see how things were goin', sure enough. You bet I could . . .'

The shape was still there, darkening now. A rider, wondered Connell. More than one? The townsmen? He shook the sweat from his face, settled his focus, concentrated.

'. . . scumbags, that's what they were. Not a constructive thought between them. All greed and grab and no brain to see it through. Take that sono-fabitch Stock.'

But by now Prof's voice had faded to a steady drone again as Connell's gaze brought the shape into sharper focus. Two riders, he decided. Sitting their mounts, just waiting. Doc Merry for one. Adam Levens for the other. Hell, they must have ridden some. But what of the others? Connell swallowed painfully on his parched throat. And what now?

'. . . and that's when I figured they would all have to go.' Prof paused a moment. 'I hope you're gettin' all this, Sheriff. And don't think for a second I haven't seen them fellas up ahead. I have, for some while. So what do you suppose they're plannin', Mr Connell?'

'I'd say this is the end of your line,' croaked Connell, stumbling as he fought to keep his balance. 'Give it up now, Prof. Let the girl go. You ain't goin' to make it past them guns ranged there, and you know it. Like you say, you're a careful fella, you think things through.'

Prof reined his mount to a halt. 'So you have been listenin'.' He grinned. 'Lawmen never cease to amaze me. But, no, Mr Connell, givin' up now ain't in my nature, and perhaps not surprisingly I have a contingency plan for just such an occasion.'

His grin broadened, his eyes gleamed. 'I shoot you, right here, right now, and ride on with the girl. As simple as that. You see the logic: the men up ahead will not doubt my resolve when they see you fall. They will not dare risk their guns against the death of the girl. In those circumstances, I think I win.'

Connell's eyes narrowed as he straddled the sand,

the sweat dripping from his chin, the sun's blaze like a fire across his back. 'You reckon?' he croaked again, his stare steady, unblinking.

'I reckon, Mr Connell,' smiled Prof. 'And just to prove the point and not waste any more time . . .'

Prof had drawn his Colt and was levelling it at Connell when the sheriff struck. A hand fell across Prof's leg in an iron grip, dragging the man from his saddle in a jumble of flailing arms and legs. The derby fell to the ground and was trampled instantly by the snorting, bucking mount.

The Colt slithered from Prof's hand; Connell kicked it aside and struck out, the clenched fist thudding into Prof's shoulder as he swayed aside.

'Not so easy, Sheriff, not so easy,' gasped Prof, scrambling for the Colt.

Connell lashed out with a vicious kick that bit into Prof's side, then rushed on again to reach for the gun, at the same time rasping out his cries for Jessie to ride. 'Head for the border,' he yelled. 'Doc's waitin'.'

He stumbled again through the drifts of sand, then fell flat on his face at Prof's sudden push and lunge, the dirt filling his mouth like the surge of a tide.

He heard the click of the gun hammer and did not dare to move.

TWENTY-SIX

'That's what comes of bein' smart,' hissed Prof, heaving for his breath as he prodded the Colt at its target. 'On your feet. I want to see your face when I pull this trigger!'

Connell came upright, blinking the sand clear of his eyes, took in the sweating, seething lump of Prof and looked round desperately for Jessie. Her mount had taken no more than a few scuffed steps forward in spite of Connell's calls for the girl to ride. What the hell, he cursed on a gasping breath, what did he have to do to make her ride?

'Jessie!' he shouted as loudly as his choking throat would permit 'F'cris'sake shift if you want us to live!'

It was then that Prof spun round to face the girl, groaning and grunting as he watched her spur her horse into action and race towards the shimmering haze of the border.

'Sonofabitch!' spat Prof, the Colt blazing wildly. He spun again, this time to face Connell.

The sheriff had lunged forward at the first hint of

Jessie's mount moving, his hands reaching like fevered claws for Prof's legs. Now, with a thudding, scrambling final effort, he flung Prof back to the sand, the Colt spinning from the man's grip under the impact of the crash.

Connell fought like a caged mountain leopard that had suddenly broken free, his fists pounding mercilessly into Prof's neck, body, face, wherever there was space for his grazed, bloody knuckles to land.

Prof struggled, squirmed, twisted first one way, then the other. But it was Connell's sudden lunge for the Colt only feet away that settled the issue.

'On your feet, rat!' ordered the sheriff, standing over Prof with the barrel of the gun levelled and steady for a shot between his eyes. 'Like I said, end of the line. Now you can get to philosophizin' on the hangman's rope!' Connell grinned slowly through his sweat. 'It just ain't been your day, has it?'

'Never thought I'd live to see the day. Sure as hell never thought I'd live to be a part of it!' Eli smacked his lips, pushed at the brim of his hat and settled to the easy pace of his mount.

'More than one of us will go along with them sentiments,' smiled Sheriff Connell, his gaze narrowing against the desert glare. 'You did a good job there, Eli. Joinin' up with Marshal Reid's posse out of Gentry in the hills was smart thinkin'. We owe you.'

'Heck, weren't nothin' along of what yourself and the others have been through, 'specially young Jessie and Miss Abigail. They goin' to be all right, Mr Connell?'

'Doc's ridin' along of both of them right now. Jessie's started to talk and take an interest, and as for Abigail . . . Abigail will always be our Abigail: up there and fightin' fit.'

'That's our gal!' grinned Eli.

'Know somethin',' said Adam Levens, trailing quietly alongside the sheriff, 'I ain't seen no finer sight than that marshal takin' in that scumbag Prof and promisin' him nothin' less than the noose once they hit Gentry again.'

'And a big amen to that,' quipped Eli. 'Thanks to the sheriff here.'

'Goes with the job, Eli,' said Connell, his gaze moving steadily across the horizon. 'Marshal Reid and his prisoner will be through the Bluespecks in four days, and Prof will be hangin' high inside the month. The rest are dead. Jessie's goin' to be fine and we're ridin' back to town with the money stolen from us. Seems like justice all round.'

'And another amen to that,' smiled Adam. 'Not that I figure for life in Bandyrock ever bein' the same again, certainly not for me and Doc. Hell, how on earth we ever managed to reach the border when we did and then just sit there in the stiflin' heat not knowin' whether to help our sheriff or not for fear of Jessie's life . . . Well, I shall never know.'

'But you did it, and the right thing too,' said Connell. He adjusted his hat against the glare. 'Suggest you two ride on ahead to join up with Wheeler and Jay. Give 'em the good news, eh? I'll ride along of Doc and his patients. Nice and easy. We ain't in no hurry, not any more.'

159

Connell reined away, waved at Doc and took a long, last look at the southern border already retreating into the haze.

Then he simply turned his back on it.